"Blast him!"

Macklowe took another careful step back until his heel touched the sidewalk. There was no obvious cover within ten yards in any direction. He was an unobstructed target. The rifle in his right hand felt suddenly heavy, his palms wet with perspiration.

"One Macklowe is as good as another!" Pearce called out as he raised the scattergun.

His partner Brawley lifted his own pistol from its scabbard.

Macklowe stood stock still for a split second, then dove to his left, hitting the ground hard as the shotgun exploded. Hot pellets bit into the street where he had stood, kicking up a dust storm as the gun blast echoed through the town square. . . .

BIG HORN

by Greg Tobin

BALLANTINE BOOKS • NEW YORK

Library of Congress Catalog Card Number: 89-91724

ISBN 0-345-36110-5

Manufactured in the United States of America

First Edition: November 1989

This one is for my sister Mimi,
finally . . . and in haste.

ABSAROKA COUNTY, WYOMING TERRITORY. 1882.

FOR CENTURIES IT HAD BEEN THE LAND OF THE CROWS, who hunted the buffalo and the elk and found life to be good, until the advent of the Sioux, who ruled from their war ponies for a brief time, then were driven away forever, after a fight not to be forgotten, by the bluecoat soldiers.

A Jesuit missionary, a protégé of the great De Smet, came to a hill overlooking a brace of creeks that converged like the wings of a great bird and saw in his mind a city rising from the valley floor in the bosom of the mountains.

He called the city Saint Mary after the Mother of God and constructed a rude church of cottonwood logs amid a scatter of houses and stores built by enterprising whites when the territory had been pacified once and for all. The Jesuit died shortly after his church was finished. He was buried beneath the altar, and the town, which would never grow to be the city of his vision, honored him by taking the name he had given it.

The timber men came, then the cattlemen. Settlers came and stayed in the welcoming town that promised a secure, healthy life for their children. In three years, from 1878 to 1881, Saint Mary attracted two hundred new residents. In the first general election, the town was voted county seat, and a courthouse was promptly built on a knoll at American and Goose streets. The first sheriff of Absaroka County took office and was charged with enforcing the laws of town, county, territory, and nation.

Those men who respected the law found a good life for themselves and their families in Saint Mary. And those who respected no law and no man found trouble in the Land of the Crows.

CHAPTER 1

THE GIRL HAD TAKEN THE NAME MARIE LE VIEUX AT MISS Julia's insistence, but it was just as false as everything else in this life. The girl sat on the edge of the soft down mattress in a small room dimly aglow from a tinted lamp burning atop a chest of drawers that contained everything she owned. The girl sat with her hands in her lap contemplating how she was going to do it, for it was now a question of how, not if. She had made up her mind.

Her real name was Dorothy Lewis and she was seventeen years old. She wore blue silk pajamas that Miss Julia said had been made in China and shipped to this place at great expense. Miss Julia expected her girls to be grateful for all the "extras" they got in her employ. In point of fact, Miss Julia's girls were a well-fed, rarely abused, contented lot—except, that is, for Dorothy Lewis from Manhattan, Kansas. She had come here to escape the righteous boredom of her parents' Rock of Ages Baptist home. God, please forgive me, she prayed, not believing that God or anybody else could or would forgive offenses of such magnitude. She did not believe she would go to hell, but there was no heaven for a depraved, rotten girl like her, either. There was only oblivion, and that would be a blessing, a divine relief, in itself.

She shifted, lifted her legs onto the mattress, and sat Indian-style, looking out the window. She pressed her fingers against the cold glass. There, across the narrow

3

street she saw a man who held a book in one hand and held the other hand above his head. He was talking, but she could not hear him, for her window was closed to keep the October chill from reaching inside her small room to touch her. She could not stand to be touched by anyone or anything anymore. No one would ever touch her again.

Over the roof of the squat building fronting the street she saw the lighted windows of several homes, and beyond, the foothills that rolled into eternal darkness.

She had never been inside one of those houses, or any other building than the one she was in—Miss Julia's house. She had never purchased a dress or a hat, never eaten a meal in a café, never attended Sunday service in the whitewashed church at the southeast corner of town. She had never felt that she belonged in this place. Always a visitor, an outsider, when what she wanted most was to be a part of the world that she saw passing her window every day and night, to take her place among these people, and to earn their respect. Why else had she come so far from home and sold herself—soiled herself—to survive in a world very different from the one she saw from her window?

Dorothy Lewis rose from the bed and went to the bureau, opened a drawer, and carefully removed a white dress. It was her mother's wedding dress; she had taken it with her when she ran away from home over a year ago and had kept it in the hope of one day wearing it at her own wedding. She put it on, with some difficulty, for it was slightly too small. Her mother had been a dainty bride. Dorothy had put on some weight at Miss Julia's request. Miss Julia said men liked plump girls.

She sobbed as she looked at herself in the cracked, rusted mirror over the washbasin. Once she had considered herself pretty. In fact, she had been rather vain; her mother had punished her more than once for standing before the mirror and admiring herself. Tonight she saw nothing to admire. The honey-tinted hair was dingy and uncombed, the eyes had dulled and were puffy from tears. She choked back a sob. She wished someone, one of the other girls, would knock at her door. She wanted to talk to somebody.

She remembered her last argument with her mother, a few weeks before she ran away. After dinner, as Dorothy washed the dishes and her parents sat at the table, her mother had said, "You were talking with Mr. Harrison's son today when I was at the market."

"He asked me if he could escort me to the social next Saturday."

The woman's raw, red hands came together and she lifted her gaze toward the low ceiling of the frame house. "God, save my daughter from her sinful, selfish ways."

"But, Mother, it is only a social. I didn't even say I would go. I told him I'd ask you and Father."

"Men are corrupt and not to be countenanced."

"But you and Father—"

"We are married, sanctified in the eyes of God. It is different then. But no less unpleasant."

"What do you mean, Mother? I do not understand."

"Women are the fairer sex, and if the truth be known, the stronger. Men like to think they give the orders and run things—but that is only because we let them. You must understand this, daughter: Men are stupid creatures, ruled by lust and greed. This is our advantage over them."

"But Father is a righteous man."

"Oh, he tries very hard to control the animal instincts, child. But sometimes it becomes too much even for him. Then I am called upon to bear his beastly advances. By God's grace I have borne five children through this disgraceful coupling, and I know not if I shall have to bear more. It is God's will, child, not for our understanding."

Dorothy saw clearly in her mind her mother's iron-gray hair that always stubbornly escaped her Sunday hat in snaky tendrils. Her mother's eyes: blue chips that reflected the righteous fire of her soul. The face: wide and high-cheekboned with a dark eyebrow that bridged her nose, a deep cleft in the forehead, flesh-padded jowls. Her mother rarely looked directly at her; rather, she gazed heavenward in perpetual supplication for her sinning husband and children, especially this daughter who dreamed about pretty dresses and Saturday-night dances and long-legged men with dark eyes.

"You must pray for your salvation, daughter. You must pray every day and every night that the Lord will have mercy upon your soul."

"But I do pray. I have done nothing wrong—nothing to be punished for."

"I see the restlessness in you, the doubt, the curiosity about men. You are of an age when your body is changing—the devil's handiwork. And you must seek God's mercy, or else you will be prey to the Evil One. I see it in you, child, and I fear for your soul."

Dorothy's father sat silently at the table reading his Bible by the light of an oil lamp. A thread of black smoke escaped the glass. He raised his eyes over the gilt-edged pages and looked at her.

The girl threw down a wet plate and it shattered on the floor. She went to her room, a cubbyhole that accommodated a bed and a small wardrobe and nothing else.

That night, when his wife was sleeping, Dorothy's father came into her room. Later, when he was gone, she sponged the blood from her legs. She knew then that she must leave. The night of the social she was gone—for good.

A month later she arrived in Saint Mary and looked for a job. She found nothing. She had no money for a hotel room. Wearing a dust-rimed dress and carrying everything she owned in a flower-patterned carpetbag, she went to Miss Julia's house.

"My, my, you are a lost lamb. Come in, girl. What's your name? Where are you from? How on earth did you find your way to this little speck on the map? You can't weigh ninety pounds. What did you say your name was? Are you seeking a position? I just happen to have an opening: one of my girls got married. Isn't that sweet? Business is good, even out here in the middle of absolute nowhere.

Wild Indians, mind you. So I do need a new girl. Stand up straight, let Julia have a look. Put that grip down. Are you hungry? I am an excellent cook. All the girls say so. Never any leftovers at my table, never a hungry girl. Well, how do you like that? Come, it's nearly suppertime. What's your name, dear?"

In the dining room, with three other girls who looked her up and down and sideways, she ate her first real meal in weeks, and she slept through the following day.

The countless miles and numbing changes melted from her memory: her journey without a destination had come to an end. She dreamed of returning home, saw it like a melodrama on a stage, every line delivered by the actors familiar and tragic. The pain in the deepest, most intimate part of her ebbed—but it did not desist completely.

Miss Julia came to her room and spoke to her, offered Dorothy a temporary job as a housekeeper if she wanted to stay and earn some money before she moved on. Where was she headed?

Dorothy had no answer. She knew what lay behind Miss Julia's offer, knew what decision she was really being asked to make. There was no alternative.

"You won't regret it, my dear. I made the choice thirty years ago, before you were even born, and I cannot imagine what it would have been like otherwise. I have seen so much of the world! Chicago, Toronto, New Orleans, Denver. I even spent a winter in the Yukon in a two-room shack with nine white men and one Indian. They were drunk most of the time and did not bother me much. The Indian—a Nez Percé, he claimed anyway—was a perfect gentleman. I won't let any man hurt one of my girls, no matter how much money he has. And it's usually the ones with money who are the meanest. I never married, but most of my girls have. Some of them left me to open their own houses. The only thing I ask is that you move at least fifty miles away to open your own house. Otherwise, I won't keep any girl here against her will. Don't cry, dear, it's a good life. What do you want? To get married to a nice

7

young man? To get rich? To buy a dress shop? You can do whatever you want with your life—except become a schoolteacher. But that's about all you can't do. Do you like this room? It'll be yours. Nice bed, new wardrobe chest, a window for fresh air. Sometimes it's a bit noisy, being over the street. I asked the sheriff if he would do something about the noise—mostly drunken cowboys—and he promised he would try. Nice man, Sheriff White-law, a widower. You must meet that handsome young deputy. He's been one of my best customers, very sweet to the girls, and generous—a real gentleman."

She no longer had her own name. Miss Julia's picture of the world had proved to be farfetched, though the girl did not doubt the woman's good intentions. Yes, she had met the deputy—and the deputy's brother.

The brother was no gentleman; he was rough with her sometimes. In bed with him she discovered her own wan-tonness. When she was with him, she felt like a complete, grown-up woman. When he was gone, she became the sad, sinful little girl whose own mother despaired of her. She thought she loved him. But where was he? He had left nearly three months ago. No word. Even his brother did not know where he had gone.

She wanted to talk to somebody before it was too late.

No, I don't want to talk to anybody, except maybe him. . . . But he will not come back to me. He is like all the other men. Yet what was it he had said once? "You are too delicate for this life, Marie." Had he meant it, or was it just love talk? It was rare that a man spoke at all, let alone such tender-sounding words.

She hugged her arms to her breast. The white dress smelled of hope. Why do I feel this way? Is it my own fault? I have sinned, yes, but I was led into this life against my will. Even he sees this. He knows I am not a whore, I am a good girl, I was raised properly but I ran away because I could not take it anymore, the smother-ing, the preaching, the deadness, no love, no under-standing, nothing.

But even as she remembered the bleak life she had fled, she wished she could go back—and knew that she could never return.

In the wedding dress, she walked around the bed and picked up the stockings she had dropped on the floor. She tied the stockings together in a tight little knot and looked around the room.

Where? There was only one place: the bedpost. If she tied one end to the post . . . the length would have to be just right: she could roll from the bed, fall to the floor . . . would it work that way?

She tied one end of the stockings securely to the bedpost and held the other in her moist palm, looked at it. Dear Lord, forgive me. She sat upon the bed once again. She believed God would forgive her, somehow, though it went against everything she had been taught. But what would *he* think? She decided to leave a letter. She had paper in the chest next to the bed, and pen and ink.

Her eyes were clouded as she dipped the pen point in the inkbottle. She began to write: "Dearest Love—" She poured out her heart, filled two pages in a wild hand.

When the ink was dry, she folded the pages once and wrote his name on the outside and left the letter on the bed.

The wind rattled the window. The girl lifted her trembling hands to her face to wipe away the tears. She fixed the other end of the stocking around her neck, then she fell into a pillow and wept.

CHAPTER 2

BEYOND HER WINDOW, IN THE WIND-WHIPPED STREET below, the man with the book ignored the cold lash upon his face. He had a mission: "The Angel Moroni spake unto me in words terrible to utter, more terrible to hear. The time of tribulation is upon us and the unrighteous will perish in fire and stand before Jehovah to be judged for their sins, thence condemned to the pit, where they shall writhe in pain and agony forever—unless they repent and change their ways and come to God. For He hath revealed Himself to the prophet and revealed His Kingdom and revealed the Way."

The holy man looked more like a ghost than a prophet: with a gauzy black beard on his haggard brown face and eyes that burned with blue heat. He did not wear a hat and his wispy hair blew every which way. He did wear a long black coat, unbuttoned, and wrinkled corduroy trousers held in place by a rope at the waist. His boots were scuffed, almost heelless. His mouth continued working.

"For it is written: In the latter days . . . the Antichrist shall come amongst the people and ye shall know him by his works. Nation shall make war upon nation, man shall lift hand against man, the unclean shall make unclean laws, and the fornicator shall rule the sons and daughters of the unconsecrated."

Behind the wind-whipped prophet, a slender dark figure moved in the shadows. He stepped along the sidewalk

10

quietly, precisely, in a military gait. He was in no hurry as he observed the stranger. He stopped several yards from the preacher and leaned against a wall.

He reached into his coat and took out a ready-made cigarette, lit it with a wooden match, and drew the smoke deeply into his lungs. He stood there quietly for a moment, listened to the man who had no idea he had a close-up audience.

"The Whore of Babylon shall spawn this Antichrist and the Earth will be overrun with the Legions of Darkness, for God has despaired of His people. Woe be unto the evil-doers and those who speak not and act not against evil and sinfulness."

The voice lifted eerily onto the wind and carried down the street where a few people glanced up before going about their normal business.

"And the Lord's anger shall be kindled, and the heathen shall tremble, and the shadow of death shall be upon them that do not believe!"

The watcher moved from the shadows to where the prophet stood and put a hand upon his shoulder. The man spun, raising the book, a battered Bible, and glared.

"Who are you?" The eyes burned feverishly.

"I am Ben Macklowe, deputy sheriff of Absaroka County, and you, sir, are whom?"

"You have no jurisdiction over the Lord's servant. I was sent here by the president and prophet of the true church, Brother Brigham Young, to bring the revealed Word to the heathen of Wyoming."

"I have no doubt, but I must ask you to desist at this hour when the good people of this village are in their homes preparing supper and at peace with the world."

"There will be no peace until they heed the Word."

"They can heed it tomorrow," Macklowe suggested.

"I will establish a mission church here. There is a time of tribulation approaching." The gaunt, grizzled specter pointed a bony yellow finger at the deputy sheriff. Macklowe was surprised to see that he was actually quite young

—probably not yet thirty years old. "The Angel Moroni hath spake unto me—terrible, terrible words—"

"I know, I heard that part. Move along now. You have a place to sleep?"

"Like the lilies of the field—"

"You neither reap nor sow. Well, just stay out of trouble, sir. Good night." Macklowe tipped his narrow-brimmed black hat to the stranger and walked toward the center of town.

Saint Mary was populated by about five hundred souls —some more in need of saving than others, no doubt— most of whom worked in some way or another to support the cattle business that was omnipresent in this section of the world. Beneath the Big Horn mountains, in a wide, fertile valley that stretched farther than a lone man could ride in a day, hundreds of thousands of head were raised on a number of large outfits that circled Saint Mary like the orbits of so many giant planets. This autumn in particular had seen a healthy harvest, and there was money being spent in Saint Mary, cowmen getting drunk in Saint Mary, and need in Saint Mary for extra law, like Ben Macklowe, deputy sheriff.

Macklowe had been here for six months. He had hired on at the invitation of a former Confederate sergeant with whom he had served, who was now the sheriff. He tossed the burning cigarette into the street and pulled his coat closer.

Six months: uneventful, quiet, strangely exhilarating after thirty-odd years of drifting and fighting other men's wars. He had been from Canada to Mexico, from Broadway in New York to San Francisco's loudest, gaudiest saloons, he had been called a no-good and a whoremaster, a friend and an enemy by many men. This was a different life for Ben Macklowe, and he liked it.

There was the girl at Miss Julia's, for whom he felt responsible: a sad, pretty thing, awfully young, eager to be his friend because she loved his elder brother.

He consulted his watch: nearly eight P.M. His shift

ended at midnight. He would see Jain tonight.

At thirty-seven, Macklowe cut a trim, neat figure in his tailored suits and jaunty, brushed hats. Tonight he wore a black suit and black tie over a crisp boiled white shirt. His overcoat was gray, with pearl-inlaid buttons, perhaps a bit too fancy for Saint Mary, but, hell, that was Ben Macklowe, and that's what they got for their money.

The sheriff, Claude Whitelaw, didn't give a damn how his deputies dressed—and some of them in years past gave a new flavor to the word *slovenly*—as long as they were on time and did not drink on duty. That could be difficult, the not-drinking part, but Macklowe was smart enough and disciplined enough to follow the rules. Besides, he needed the job.

In the past few years he had seen a lot of money pass through his hands at the gaming tables, but very little of it had stayed in his pocket for long. So, as much as he hated the idea of it, he was working for wages, and as it had turned out, it was not so bad at all.

He held no affection for Saint Mary and its people. He merely did his job as efficiently as he could, expected no thanks or special treatment merely because he wore a county badge. He was learning this law enforcement business as he went; there wasn't much to it after all.

Near the square, where the county courthouse, sheriff's headquarters and jail, the Grand Central Hotel, two taverns, and a Congregational church faced each other serenely if incongruously, Macklowe stopped again and peered down the dark streets that converged there.

All was quiet. He cut across the square where a naked flagpole stood watch to the headquarters of the sheriff of Absaroka County, his employer.

He sat at the front desk after a cursory check of the three cells in back, no one there. He felt fine, poured himself a cup of bitter black coffee, lukewarm now after being reheated several times during the day. He was thinking, Not such a bad place to be—when there was a commotion outside and the front door slammed open.

His colleague, fellow-deputy Matthew Drayton, hauled a big man inside and kicked the door shut. Drayton made straight for the backroom cells as Macklowe watched with amused disinterest. Another night, another drunk. Then he caught a glimpse of the drunk's face and sat up straight.

The drunk, a tall, broad-shouldered, long-necked man with unkempt black hair, was oblivious to his surroundings, half-asleep with a stupid grin on his stubbled face. He did not look up from the floor.

Macklowe waited until Drayton came back out front.

"Had to disarm the son of a bitch." He dropped a black Colt Peacemaker on the desk in front of Macklowe. "Log that in for me, please, Ben."

Macklowe liked Drayton well enough: a young man with a pretty wife and daughter. Such a life didn't seem so bad close-up and he did not sneer inwardly anymore as he had at first. He was getting open-minded in his old age.

Drayton went out and Macklowe went back to the cells. It was dark and smelled of sweat and urine and he hated it. He had been in a Mexican prison once that was a hundred times worse than this crackerbox, but the mere idea of jail made him uncomfortable.

The man in the cell lay on his back, his limbs overhanging the rickety cot. He snored. He reeked disgustingly of whiskey and perspiration and despair. The deputy sheriff gripped the cold bars and pressed his face between them.

"Reede," he said. The corpselike thing did not respond. "Reede," he said again. "Wake up."

This time the drunken man stirred and one eye slowly opened. Suddenly he was sitting bolt upright, staring like a madman at Ben Macklowe. "What the hell—" He squinted as if there were a blinding glare emanating from Macklowe's face. "It is—brother Ben. How the hell are you, son?"

"I'm doing just fine. I won't ask you the same question."

"Hell, man, I came here to see you and here you are. I count that a success. How the hell did I get in here?"

"You tell me. Another man brought you in. You must have been causing trouble somewhere."

Reede Macklowe sat on the end of the cot with his hands on his knees, looking up at the nattily attired lawman. "It is good to see you, kid."

"Unexpected is the word. How did you track me here?" He passed a lit cigarette through the bars and lit one for himself. Inhaling it through his nostrils he blocked out the stink of his brother and the cell.

"Word gets around. I was down in San Antonio, making out pretty nice, living with a Mexican gal for a couple of weeks—real sweet, drank wine like a baby drinks milk— and got into a scrape, had to move fast, figured I'd go north for a change. Heard about you from some cow people in Ellsworth."

"I'll be damned. It's good to see you, Reede."

"So you're wearing a star now. Looks smart. Nice racket."

"I am new to the law game since you left."

"It's like any other: the smart ones survive and live to fight another day. I thought about doing it once myself."

"You better get some sleep. We'll talk in the morning."

"Think you can get me out of this one, kid? Seeing as you're the law in this town."

"I'll talk to Sheriff Whitelaw. He's a good egg."

"Don't mention food." Reede Macklowe curled up on the cot and instantly passed out.

Ben Macklowe thought about the wild-eyed prophet he had shooed along earlier and considered saying a prayer for his drunken brother.

Instead he returned to the desk out front and wrote a note to Whitelaw asking for his brother's release into his custody once Reede had sobered up.

Whitelaw had never liked the elder Macklowe brother, thought him a wastrel and a bad influence upon Ben.

"For Christ's sake, I'm a grown man, Claude," Ben had said.

"Doesn't mean he can't ruin your life," Whitelaw said.

"You and him are cut from the same stubborn Scotch cloth. I know. I served with you in the late war, in case you have forgot."

Macklowe had not forgot. He had held the rank of first lieutenant in the Second Kentucky Cavalry Regiment under the command of John Hunt Morgan. Whitelaw had been a sergeant of horse—and a damned good one in his day.

As HE LEFT THE OFFICE AFTER MIDNIGHT, MACKLOWE breathed in the icy air, pulled his hat lower, more snugly onto his head. His hand touched the revolver he wore in a crossdraw rig on his right hip. He buttoned the top button on his coat, then pulled on a pair of leather gloves. All was quiet in Saint Mary tonight—since his brother was sleeping it off in jail.

He passed Miss Julia's house and noticed a light on in "Marie's" window. He wondered what her real name was. She would be pleased that Reede had come back, no matter how pitiful the shape he was in. Why she felt so strongly about him, Macklowe could not figure. Then again, he felt pretty strong about Jain. Maybe it was the same thing. Maybe it just did not matter to the girl that Reede was a drunk and a brawler with no future.

He had left Saint Mary several months ago owing several large gambling debts, promising to make enough to repay them. Macklowe doubted Reede had returned with any assets. If he had accumulated anything in Galveston, he had drunk it away by now, for certain. He had come back because there was nowhere else to go.

Jain Dobbie's was the last house on Second Street, a two-room frame structure surrounded by an unpainted fence. Macklowe had promised he'd paint it but somehow hadn't found the time. Whenever he was at Jain's—most often at night—he spent most of his time in her bed.

She opened the door and he stepped inside. She closed the door behind him and turned to embrace him.

Macklowe took her slender form into his arms and put his cheek against hers. Her hair smelled of rose-scented soap. It was both coarse and soft in his face. She raised her eyes and looked into his.

Jain Dobbie had deep brown eyes and brown skin, black hair, and beautifully high, slanted cheekbones. Her full lips opened to reveal perfect white teeth. She stood on her tip-toes to kiss him.

He felt her hunger and clung tightly to her. He lifted her and carried her to the bedroom, where they lay together for a long time without speaking a word; they explored each other, kissing, slowly freeing themselves of clothing.

A fragment of light from the oil lamp in the sitting room fell across the bed. Later, he got up and put his long johns back on. Jain draped a robe over her shoulders.

She said, "You are a bad boy."

"I have given up trying to be good."

Jain Dobbie laughed musically. "I wouldn't want you if you were good. I like you bad."

"Are you my friend?" Macklowe asked.

She sat up straight and raked a small hand through the black tangle of hair that fell over her dark eyes. The robe covered her breasts but not the long dusky shadowed neck. He had kissed that neck hundreds of times.

"That is a strange and silly question. Of course, I am your friend. We were friends before we became—" She looked away with becoming modesty. As lusty and hungry as Jain was in bed, she acted every inch the lady, publicly and privately. "Before we went to bed," she finished.

Macklowe remembered their first meeting. He took two of his three shirts to her laundry on the recommendation of Claude Whitelaw. "Damn good laundress. Quiet girl, pretty. None of her kind round here to marry, I suppose."

She was a damn good laundress and Macklowe began to take all his clothes to her for washing and repair. She was not a bad seamstress, either. They became friendly, and he felt at ease around her.

Jain Dobbie had been in Saint Mary for three years. She had worked for a short time at Miss Julia's house but was hurt once by a trail bum and quit. She opened her own laundry and built up a good, steady business. She minded her own affairs. She avoided men—until Ben Macklowe came around. Jain liked what she saw from the beginning, but she waited for him to take the first step.

How it happened was strange. But, then, she soon got used to Macklowe's certain brand of strangeness.

"I am married," he said one day. "But I haven't seen my wife in about three years. She lives in Austin. I never did like that town."

"Why are you telling me this?" Jain said.

"I don't want to start out lying to you. Would you like to have supper with me tonight? I quit work at six o'clock."

"Yes. Why don't you come to my house. I will fix supper. I haven't had anybody—man or woman—inside my house since I moved there."

That's how they had started. Reede, who had met Jain once during his previous sojourn in Saint Mary, said, "She's good looking. A bit on the dark side, eh?"

Macklowe said, "Shut your mouth. You have your whores, but I'm a married man. I need a good, quiet woman, a friend more than anything else."

"You're an odd one, Ben," his brother said.

Now, Ben Macklowe walked across the cold floor of Jain's house in his bare feet to put some more wood in the stove. Outside, the wind howled against the frame house. He came back to her bed.

"Are you hungry?" she asked.

"No. Reede is back in town. Drunk and in jail."

"That's where he belongs. I look at him and cannot believe he's your brother. He's so different from you, Ben." She touched his face. "Has he been to see that poor girl at Julia's?"

"Not yet. He will when he sobers up tomorrow."

"He won't be sober tomorrow. Not for a year of tomorrows. He's a bad drunk."

"I drink too much, too," Macklowe said. In fact, he had a strong craving for a drink at that moment. "It runs in the family."

"Come here." She opened her arms and he went to her. She held his head to her breast, stroking his hair.

"I'm surprised you haven't thrown me out, girl."

"No, I haven't. Not yet. If you get too bad I will, believe me. I don't tolerate improper behavior in white folks. My mother taught me that much."

"Thank God for your mother."

"Ben, I have something to tell you." She held him more tightly to her.

He waited, listening to her breathing, taking in the smell and feel of her. He was falling in love with this woman and it worried him somewhat. A man in his position, in a town like Saint Mary . . . it was absurd. Yet he could not, would not deny what he felt.

"I'm going to have a baby," she said. "Your baby, Ben."

CHAPTER 3

THE ORANGE CAT WITH GRAY EYES SIDLED ALONG THE wall at the far side of the room. Whitelaw watched the animal in the mottled mirror as he shaved.

On this November morning, it had taken every bit of energy he possessed to get out of bed and face the cat, let alone the rest of the world. I'm getting awfully damned old, he thought, looking at the sagging face in the mirror.

He dressed, straining to button his trousers, cursing his big, round belly. Didn't use to be this way. Used to be a man could fit his own trousers.

The orange cat leaped onto Whitelaw's rumpled bed and made a place for himself there in a valley of sheets. All the while he watched the struggles of the man who now sat and pulled his boots on, then stood and caught his breath.

He would skip breakfast this morning, but he needed some coffee to open his eyes. He went downstairs to the kitchen of the rooming house where he made his home and drank a full cup in a few gulps. After bringing a bowl of cream upstairs for the cat, he left the house for the short walk to work.

Saint Mary was not a bad place to be, he often reminded himself. The big cattle spreads in the valley were the focus of economic activity, and they kept the folks in town and county clothed and fed.

Claude Whitelaw was a robust, if somewhat overweight sixty years old with ruddy skin and stark white hair, the sheriff moved stiffly across the square to his office. His left leg was shorter than his right because it had been shattered in the war, causing a pronounced limp that, like his signature, identified him wherever he went.

Whitelaw had never married, and after the war he had come to Wyoming to live with his brother who lived with wife and children on a small spread near town. The brother was now dead, the sister-in-law removed to Powell, Illinois, and the kids married and scattered throughout Wyoming and Utah. Whitelaw was alone, and he was well used to it by now.

He lived in the rooming house and minded his own business—and the cat's—and it suited him. He had a few friends, a few books, and a few worries to keep him company when he desired it.

He had not reached the office when he caught sight of Miss Julia Mayer striding toward him. She was a tall woman, big in all the right places, according to Claude Whitelaw, and she moved swiftly across the street. She was out of breath when she reached him.

"Claude, one of my girls—" She gulped air and held a frayed shawl tightly around her shoulders. "She's dead. Young Marie—Dorothy."

"Did you call for a doctor?"

"No need. She's dead as a doornail. Cold and stiff. She—I think she killed herself."

Whitelaw followed the madam five long blocks to her house and upstairs. There he saw the lovely alabaster corpse in the wedding gown, her face mortally contorted.

He helped Julia lift the girl from the floor and place her on the bed. The coroner, Dr. Robert Justich, who was equally adept at delivering babies, setting broken horse bones, and courting votes, rather redundantly pronounced Dorothy Lewis dead and asked the sheriff to witness the certificate. Miss Julia Mayer served fresh coffee to the two officials in her parlor.

Justich said, "Such a pretty girl. Had she seemed disturbed, Julia?"

"No, she was always a quiet one. Didn't have any close friends among the other girls."

"Did she leave a letter?" Whitelaw asked.

"Would you care for more coffee, doctor?" Julia lifted the coffeepot.

"No thank you, I must be going. Claude, Miss Julia." He put on his hat and hefted his medical bag.

"I had better get to my desk, too," Whitelaw said. "You didn't answer my question, Julia."

"I know I didn't, Claude. Come back later, please."

He looked at her, trying to puzzle her meaning, then gave up. He had long ago learned that women could not be—should not be—figured out.

Whitelaw was wiping his brow as he stepped into his office a short time later. Ben Macklowe was asleep in a chair in the corner. He wondered why the hell the man had not gone home after his shift and slept in a proper bed. But that was Ben Macklowe. He had probably been up half the night at his girlfriend's house. Whitelaw did not approve of his deputy's love affair with the beautiful mulatto girl, but neither did he vocally disapprove. It was a man's own business.

Whitelaw remembered a younger, recklessly brave, almost uncontrollable Ben Macklowe in those bloody, bygone days with the Second Kentucky Cavalry Regiment under Brigadier General John Hunt Morgan. Macklowe had started as a young lieutenant and finished his service as a major; Whitelaw had begun—and finished—as a sergeant of horse in the "fashionable" unit with the courtly cavalier commander.

The regiment lasted less than three years and saw some of the wildest fighting of the war. Macklowe had drifted in from Canada—he said—seeking to join the fight that he had no real stake in. Whitelaw had been born poor and raised up poor in Perryville, Kentucky. He got on with horses from an early age and worked around the central part of the state first as a stable boy, then as race trainer, and when Morgan needed horsemen for his high-flying cavalry regiment, Whitelaw was one of the first to sign up. He most certainly had a stake in the conflict between the Union and the Confederate states.

Macklowe was not a natural on horseback, but he had a stubborn streak nearly as wide as his wild stripe and he lived in the saddle for the nearly three years that Morgan's unit tore up federals in those famous raids in Tennessee and Kentucky. By the time the regiment had disintegrated and Morgan was dead, Major Macklowe did not fall off his horse nearly as much as he used to.

One afternoon outside of Belton, Tennessee, on the Cumberland Plateau, the grapeshot from federal cannon had pinned down Macklowe's regiment and spooked the horses in a surprise engagement. It was a mass writhing of smoke, dust, panicked horseflesh, and the shouting of men. Major Macklowe rallied his men and sought to order them for battle.

"Sergeant Whitelaw!" he shouted, nearly choking on the soot in the air. His own mount, a roan mare, turned her head, nostrils flaring, trying to ascertain whether the rider was as insane as he seemed, not retreating from this dangerous chaos.

Whitelaw reported to the major. "Sir!" He came up on foot, saluted, awaited orders.

"Take twenty men to that wood beyond the left flank and make them stay put—no matter what. I want to hold back a small reinforcement. The rest of us are going in."

"Sir, if you go in, you'll be the only one. It's foolish, sir, if I may express my opinion."

Macklowe respected Whitelaw's military experience and his honesty. He relied heavily on the sergeant's common sense—a quality that Macklowe had little of.

"Thank you for that observation, Sergeant. Take your detachment to the woods and await my order to charge from cover."

Less than an hour later, after a valiant and decidedly foolish head-on charge into the enemy artillery positions, Macklowe disengaged his decimated force and rode to meet with the reinforcements who were waiting in the wood.

Whitelaw was relieved that Macklowe had survived the skirmish but counted at least fifteen fewer men coming out than had gone in.

Major Macklowe reined in his big roan and held up his hand, calling to his men, "Time to retreat, gentlemen. Follow me."

Macklowe's gray campaign hat was battered, his face streaked with black powder smoke, his eyes afire. Whitelaw mounted and fell in beside the major. Then, as they rode from the sheltering trees, all hell broke loose.

Balls from the federal cannon fell around them in a vicious rainstorm. The earth heaved up beneath them, vomiting mud and stone.

Macklowe wheeled his frightened mount, tried to push his men back toward the trees, but could not shout loud enough to be heard over the trumpeting horses and exploding shot. Clods of wet earth shot up before his mount. The animal reared, almost throwing him. Macklowe put a calming hand on the horse's neck, but it was no use: the animal had seen enough and bucked away.

A few men were already in the wood when the major's mount bolted in that direction. He turned in the saddle in time to see two of his men killed by a single enemy ball, falling from their horses in twisted agony. The hellish scene seared into his mind. He would never forget this, the ugly face of war.

Then he saw Sergeant Claude Whitelaw lying in the dug-up earth, horses and men swirling around him— pinned beneath his mount. Macklowe dismounted and ran onto the field to Whitelaw.

"Go away, Major!" Whitelaw waved him back, spitting out the words painfully. "Get back!"

Macklowe came on. He caught an unhorsed soldier by the shoulders and pulled the man with him. Whitelaw's left leg lay beneath the dead horse's shoulder. Macklowe strained to lift the animal while the soldier pulled Whitelaw's heavy body. The sergeant wanted to scream out in pain but bit his lip. Macklowe heaved. The horse came up enough to let Whitelaw's leg slip free.

The soldier stood and dusted his hands off and was shot dead by a long-range rifle shot. He fell beside Whitelaw.

"Let's move it, Sergeant," Macklowe said, hooking the older man by the shoulders and dragging him away from the carnage.

It was a miracle that they reached the wood without further injury. With help, Macklowe got Whitelaw onto a new mount and rode out with the survivors to rejoin General Morgan. That night the surgeons did their best to save Whitelaw's broken, bullet-shattered legs.

Outside the hospital tent Major Ben Macklowe paced back and forth in the cold, damp night until he received word from the chief surgeon that the sergeant was going to survive. He would never walk normally, but he would live.

WHITELAW SAT AT HIS PAPER-CLUTTERED DESK AND calmly lit his pipe. The man snoring in the corner had shown up in this office one day last spring looking lean and hungry and very unhappy, with a week's whiskers and a bellyful of whiskey. Whitelaw dried him out at his own house and offered him the deputy's job.

Macklowe had not accepted immediately. "Give me a day to think on it," he had said.

"Don't think so much, Major Macklowe. Get you in trouble, all that thinking."

"You have a point there, Sheriff."

For an entire day Macklowe sat in Whitelaw's kitchen drinking coffee and smoking those fancy cigarettes he liked.

When Whitelaw returned at dusk, Macklowe said, "Just don't call me 'Major' and you own yourself a deputy."

"Nobody's ever going to own you, Ben." Whitelaw was pleased that the younger man had decided to put away the gambling and gunplay to settle in Saint Mary. But he was careful to rein in the feeling for fear he would drive Mack-lowe away again.

Now he gently touched Macklowe's leg. "Wake up, son." The deputy stirred, opened his eyes. Whitelaw handed him a cup of steaming coffee. "Why didn't you get some sleep in your own bed last night?"

"Wasn't tired—then. Had some business to see to."

"You're in early, you could have slept some at home."

"Special visitor." Macklowe inclined his head toward the jail cells. He took his waterproof cigarette case from a breast pocket. He offered Whitelaw one.

"Thanks," the sheriff said, still somewhat suspicious of these manufactured, ladylike objects. But he could not deny he liked the taste of them better than the plug he smoked in his old pipe. "So, who is this guest of honor?"

"My brother Reede, up from San Antonio."

"How did he come to be invited to stay with us?"

"Drunk and disorderly. That's Reede. He is a magnet for trouble. Always has been."

"You don't have to tell me. Seems like we've been through all this before. Why did he come back to my county?"

"He heard I was still here. Needed somewhere to hang his hat, lie low. Probably could not believe his little brother was wearing a law badge after all the scrapes *I've* been in." He inhaled the tobacco and released it through his nostrils, smiling.

"Well, we're going to be plenty busy, looks like. Miss Julia just told me one of her girls hanged herself last night."

Macklowe stiffened; he instinctively knew who it was but did not understand exactly why he knew. Did it have anything to do with Reede's reappearance? It was too ugly to contemplate. There was a cold quicksilver feeling in his intestines. He looked directly at the sheriff.

"Marie," he said.

Whitelaw squinted, pulled his watch from his pocket.

26

"Let's you and me go over there, Ben. Julia's in a poor state. Told her I'd come back right away."

"She ought not be surprised. Those girls, some of them are pretty rough cases. But this one . . . did Julia do something to make her kill herself? You've known the woman longer than I have."

"She hasn't broken any laws yet. She's not a bad woman, Ben." Whitelaw tossed his cigarette into a spittoon.

Macklowe rose, stretched his arms behind hs head, and yawned. He took his hat from the desk. "She won't be happy to hear that Reede is back. You can have the honor of informing her." He placed the hat on his head at an angle. "Let's go, Sheriff."

The girl's body lay in the bed, the face drained of color except for two evil bruises beneath her eyes. She wore the wedding dress. Macklowe looked away. Whitelaw stumped around the room inspecting the contents of the bureau drawers and the closet, rearranging the items on the bed table.

"Did she leave a letter—anything?" Macklowe said.

Whitelaw muttered that Julia had found something, had not shown it to him.

"I want to see it."

"Ask Julia," the sheriff said.

Macklowe did, but Julia claimed she had burned it.

"Why the hell did you do that?"

She was nearly six feet tall, a once-beautiful courtesan who presented a hard, colorful mask to the world: flaming hennaed hair, dark brows and lashes, impossible blue eyes and maroon lips, powdered skin, extravagant dresses and gestures. Macklowe sometimes wondered how old she was, guessed about fifty, realized that it did not matter, for she was ageless, eternal, had lived forever. Like her girls who had embarked upon a life in which time ceased to matter. But sometimes the young ones, like Dorothy Lewis, could not face an eternity and ended their tenure by running away or taking their lives.

Julia had seen it before and she was as sorry for this one as she had been for the others.

"It was her private business—and mine," she stated.

"It is a matter for the law." The sheriff stood behind Macklowe. "You know better, Julia."

"I know what I know, Claude, and the law rarely has anything to do with it. This poor creature made her own choice of her own free will. If she had wanted to leave, I would not have stopped her. You know that."

Whitelaw's ample eyebrows dipped and lifted. "You are an honorable woman, but Macklowe here is right: the letter is evidence. Suicide is a crime."

"Life is a crime," Julia said.

CHAPTER 4

MACKLOWE HEARD BUT DID NOT LISTEN TO THE EXCHANGE as he went back upstairs to take a last look at the girl's body, to pay his respects. He expected her to open her eyes and apologize for causing them trouble this morning and say she hoped to see him tonight.

The last time he had seen her, three or four nights ago, she had talked more than she ever had before. Since Reede had run out, she had no one else to confide in. The men she entertained were not friends in any way, shape, or form. If she didn't loathe them, she didn't care about them or speak to them at all.

So she was glad that he had stopped by her room to see how she was doing.

"Have you heard from him?" she asked.

"No, and don't expect to."

"I don't know why I love him. I'm going to hell for it, though."

Macklowe lit a cigarette and sat back on her bed. "I do not believe in any hell other than the one we create ourselves right here and now."

"That's blasphemy," she said.

"No, it is what I believe. You believe what you like."

"I don't know what to believe. Everything is upside down. It's not like what I was taught. I was taught that what Reede and I did is a sin unless we are married."

"Marriage to my brother would be hell, that's a certainty."

"He said you are married."

"I suppose I am. Sometimes I forget."

"Where is she?"

"A long way from here."

"Any children?"

"No. That's one reason I'm here and she's there. I wanted to have a bunch of kids. She comes from a society family in St. Louis. They don't believe in having more than one or two children. Keeps the money from spreading out too much."

She is awfully pretty, he kept thinking. Reede is such an ass to leave her like this. If he didn't come back soon, who knows what might happen. Another gent might sweep her away, marry her, make her "respectable." She wanted to get out of this life, and if Reede didn't take her, someone would, sooner or later.

"I'm sure he'll be back," Macklowe lied.

"Thank you," she said vaguely, as if she were already alone. She did not look at him.

Macklowe left her some money for her time. He did not want her to get in trouble with the madam. . . .

He came back downstairs after his last viewing of the body.

Whitelaw was saying, "Was she in any trouble? I mean —diseases or expecting or something like that?" He stared hard at the frayed rug as he spoke, shifting his weight from the bad leg, clutching his belt with both hands.

"Sheriff, she was an angel compared to some of my girls. No problems. She was very quiet. Only one special friend—man, that is." Julia did not want to say any more than that.

Macklowe spoke up. "Reede spent a lot of time with her."

Whitelaw fidgeted, wheeled around on his good leg to face Macklowe directly. "Then we know who she wrote the letter to." He let the younger man off the hook. "It wasn't some respectable married man in town. No scandal, no hysterical wife to organize the do-gooders to close down the house. Give the poor girl a decent burial, Julia."

"I will, Claude."

Outside, walking back to the office, Whitelaw said, "Sorry about the girl, Ben. She was so damn young."

"I am sorry, too, but there is nothing I can do for her anymore. I wonder how Reede will take it."

Whitelaw crabbed uncomfortably along the sidewalk beside Macklowe.

As he neared retirement, Whitelaw realized he felt more for other people and less for and within himself. He had seen war and death and lawlessness in quantities enough to suck any man dry of sympathy for his fellow earthbound sufferers, but here he was, getting sad and sentimental for this man who could surely take care of himself.

It was a startling, brilliant morning: your breath misted before your face and the white sun cast long clean shadows in the street. Saint Mary was a pretty little town if you looked at it on a morning like this and did not know or particularly care what had gone on the night before.

Next item of business was his brother, Macklowe reminded himself as he sat with yet another cup of coffee, holding it to let the sludge settle to the bottom.

Whitelaw attended to paperwork at the desk. Deputies Donimiller and Drayton bustled officiously about with their badges high and shining upon their chests, department-issue revolvers perched menacingly in buffed leather scabbards.

Macklowe wore his badge inside his coat. He was not ambivalent about his new career as a lawman, but he did not want to present such a visible target so near his heart.

He opened the Saint Mary *Mercury*, the daily four-page tabloid-size newspaper, and smelled the ink and paper, which were as pungent and real to him as flowers were to other people. He had worked as a printer's devil as a youth in Toronto and would forever associate the smell and feel of newsprint with that time in his life, which was not an unhappy time. He and Reede had been scrapping partners even then.

Those days were not so long ago, yet they seemed as if they had been in another life, or had been in a book he had read about someone else.

Ben's father, Malcolm Macklowe, had taken his family from Canada to San Antonio, Texas, when Ben was a youngster. There, Ben and Reede went—or, more often, did not go—to school and learned the arts of self-defense in almost daily confrontations with other youths, mostly over taunts about their father's very heavy, very public drinking habits.

Once, at age twelve or thirteen, Ben encountered his older, taller, better-looking brother standing off four other neighborhood boys in an alley behind one of their dad's favorite taverns.

Clouds converged overhead, heavy with menace, robbing the scene of shadows. Ben came up behind the boys, who stood in a ring of menace around Reede, and he heard them mocking Malcolm Macklowe.

"Your old man stinks of the liquor," one lad was saying. "He's no good, my daddy says, and you're no good either."

Another boy shoved Reede against a pile of wet lumber, and Reede sat down hard and looked into the close faces of his tormentors.

"You are scum," he said defiantly.

At that point Ben advanced, picking up an idle barrel stave, and caved in the black head of one youth, causing the others to turn on their victim's brother.

Ben waved the stave threateningly, his feet planted and eyes darting from face to face. These three remaining boys did not impress Ben. Reede sat, stunned, where he had been pushed, paralyzed, finally understanding what was happening.

"My heroic brother," he said. He raised himself unsteadily. He casually walked up behind one of the boys and boxed his ears. The others turned but did not move toward

Reede, keeping Ben within sight. "Now you goddamn cowards will pay," he said, sneering.

Ben lifted his fists and advanced upon the largest of Reede's tormentors. The boy was a broad-shouldered redhead with great splotches of freckles across his nose. Ben aimed for that same nose and landed a powerful blow. Blood spurted and the boy staggered backward.

"Good work!" Reede called, clapping his hands. He did not see another attacker come up behind him.

The boy captured Reede in a stranglehold and wrestled him to the ground. Reede could not breathe.

Ben, meanwhile, battled yet another kid, this one armed with a length of chain and a mean snarl. Ben raised his right arm to block the swinging chain and took the stinging blow. He lowered his head and charged, knocking the boy to the ground. He grabbed for the chain. The boy swung it again, catching Ben on the ear. Ben could feel the blood start to flow.

Reede, who was fighting to release himself, to breathe, called out, "Help me, brother!"

This caused Ben to lift his opponent's head and smash it into the dirt and leap off of him to go to help Reede.

Ben snaked an arm around the boy who held Reede and tried to yank him away. The boy got angry and released Reede and turned to fight Ben. Reede fell free and gulped air, his eyes wild with relief.

Ben Macklowe swung at his enemy and missed. The other attackers had moved to the periphery of the fight and watched warily, but none dared move against Reede.

Ben's new foe was a tall, skinny black-haired kid with long arms that he used to fend off Ben's misplaced fists. Suddenly the kid ducked and came up with a right that caught Ben beneath his chin, crunching his teeth together. Ben fell, half-conscious, into the dust. When he raised his head and shook it and looked around, Reede was the only one there.

"Thanks, brother," Reede said.

That had been more than twenty years ago and Reede

was still getting himself into trouble. Ben Macklowe got the key and went back to the foul-smelling jail cell where Reede was sleeping off his hangover.

He rattled the key against the bars. "Wake up, brother. It's morning."

Reede moved slowly, reluctantly, and groaned. He pulled himself up and swung his feet onto the floor. "Where the hell am I?"

"Safe and snug in jail. Right where you belong. Come on out and have some coffee."

After he tossed down two scalding cups, Reede was somewhat coherent. "You have any whiskey—hair of the dog, friend?"

Macklowe produced a bottle from the desk. Whitelaw had gone out to appear in court and would not be back before noon.

"Why the hell did you come, Reede?"

"Wanted to get back in time to spend Christmas with my only brother." When Reede smiled, two deep dimples scored his handsome face. Even hung over, lacking a shave and a bath, he was a damn good-looking man.

Macklowe hesitated, then said, "I've got to tell you, that girl you liked, Dorothy, she died last night. Hanged herself."

Reede Macklowe buttoned his soiled shirt and stood. He went to the high window that looked out onto a side street and saw a few people walking across the square. He looked much older than thirty-nine all of a sudden. And he slumped, seemed to shrink a bit.

"Why?" he said.

"She left a letter, addressed to you probably, but Julia destroyed it."

"Why?" he repeated. "I told her I would come back. I liked that little girl. I even thought—" He rubbed his whisker stubble. "I am a stupid ass, Ben. I'm sorry."

"You don't have to be sorry for my sake. Think about that poor girl."

"You saying it's my fault?" Reede turned and his eyes blazed at Ben.

"I'm saying you need to sober up, get a bath and some food in your stomach. You can stay with me for a while."

"You still screwing that colored girl?"

Ben Macklowe stood and took three steps toward his brother. Eye to eye, he grasped Reede's dusty shirt in a tight fist. "One of these days I am going to kill you myself if you don't become a goddamned human being. Get out of my sight."

Reede held his hands to his side. He could smell the liquor stink on his own breath and did not doubt the killing capacity of his brother. He'd never seen Ben so angry. He gathered his things and left.

That night Macklowe stayed again at Jain's and Reede slept in his bed.

Macklowe lay awake in the darkness, listening to the woman's breathing, wondering about the strange process that was unfolding within her: a child, his child, was growing within her womb. He felt no sentimentality or maudlin religiosity about it, yet he acknowledged that it was a miracle. He tried to imagine the baby that would be born into this world in several months' time. What would it look like? Would it be beautiful like her? Dark- or light-skinned? Boy or girl? It thrilled and scared him.

She stirred, sensing his thoughts, put an arm over his chest, and moved closer to him.

"Go back to sleep," he said.

"Stop thinking so hard," she said. "You need to get some rest."

"I need to get the hell out of this town. I haven't seen the country in months. I haven't been on a horse or been in the mountains. This town has been closing in on me. Now with my stubborn, drunk brother back—" He put his hand over his eyes, trying to block out the thought.

Jain Dobbie said, "You can't live your brother's life for him."

"I was thinking today how we used to get into fights

with the other kids. I saved his ass more than once. Funny, he's the older brother but I'm the one who's always getting him out of trouble. He depends on me and I don't want to be in that position anymore."

"He's a grown man now. He ought to understand that."

"But he doesn't, not a damned bit of it. It's like he hasn't learned anything since he's been ten years old. He's not stupid, in fact he's a good man at heart, but he is awfully careless with other people's lives. Like that girl— In a few days he'll forget all about her."

"Ben, stop torturing yourself. Tell him to get out of town. He'll do it if you make him. Otherwise he'll drag you down with him, I know it. And I don't want that to happen to you."

"You don't like him, do you?"

"I never have. I don't care what happens to him, only to you—to us."

Ben got out of bed. He stood there naked, goose pimples running up his arms. "I need a smoke. You sleep."

An hour later he returned to bed but could not close his eyes.

CHAPTER 5

MACKLOWE PEERED ACROSS THE TABLE, THROUGH THE blue cigar smoke, at his brother. Reede held five cards in one hand and a twenty-dollar gold piece in the other. He was not drunk, though he had consumed at least a quart of mescal.

The other players, too, had drunk their share. But it was a solemn scene with no hint of pleasure or levity or fellowship among those at the table.

There were six of them altogether, and they had been playing at this table in the lobby of the Grand Central Hotel since eleven o'clock the previous night and it was now nearly five A.M. They were deadly serious, all of them except Ben Macklowe's brother.

"Bunch of goddamned cowmen with lungs full of cow dust and noses full of cow shit," he allowed. "If I can't wipe all of you out, I'm a pretty poor stud player. I'll see your ten, Strickland, and raise you ten."

Reede dropped the twenty dollars in the pot and took another drink. He had not gotten sloppy yet, except with his mouth. That was his way: whether he was winning or losing, he made certain the other players knew he was in the game.

The other players besides Ben and Reede Macklowe were John Strickland, a cattle buyer from Nebraska; Ned Brawley and Thad Pearce from Austin, who had worked the trail with Strickland and were here blowing their monthly wages; and Hinton Rettiger, brother-in-law to Macklowe's law enforcement colleague Donimiller and editor and printer of the *Mercury*.

Strickland said, "You are out of line, Macklowe, and if I was your brother, I'd tell you to shut your face."

"What do you say, brother?" Reede turned to Ben.

Ben looked up from his cards. He was exhausted because he hadn't slept more than four hours in the two days Reede had been in Saint Mary. His blue-gray eyes were bloodshot, with dark smudges beneath them. "I am not my brother's keeper."

"Somebody ought to lock him up," Strickland insisted.

"They did that already," Reede said. "Was the charge vagrancy, brother? Or disturbing the peace? Or was it public drunkenness? These fine people in this town are being well protected from me, Mr. Strickland. I wonder, can they say the same about you and your two sheep-suckers here." He swallowed some more mescal.

John Strickland had lost nearly three hundred dollars to the Macklowe brothers. He had suffered Reede's abuse for several hours in an effort to win back some of his losses. But now he threw down his cards and exploded.

"I've taken more than enough shit from you!" He glared malevolently at Reede.

Pearce and Brawley froze, emaciated statues, watching their boss, ready to react to his wrath. Rettiger, who sat between Ben and Strickland, stubbed out his cigar. He was a long-faced man with spectacles, his gray hair an unruly fringe he tried unsuccessfully to keep swept behind his large ears. He had a lantern jaw and huge, dirty hands.

He said, "Calm down, Strickland. It's only a game, man." He put a yellow-and-black-stained hand on the cowman's sleeve. Strickland pulled away his arm.

"Don't touch me, printer. You are as bad a scum as these two thieves."

Ned Pearce said, "Don't do it, Mr. Macklowe." He was looking directly at Reede, who held his left hand—his gun hand—beneath the table.

Reede Macklowe put both hands on the table and smiled crookedly. "Not me, friend. I fight fair."

"You want a fight?" Strickland demanded.

"Hold everything." Ben Macklowe got to his feet. His black tie was still neatly knotted, though his shirt had wilted during the long, close night at the table. He stood five-foot-seven in his stocking feet and his broad shoulders gave the impression that he was a bigger man. He smoothed his dark brown mustache. "There will be no fighting here. The manager will throw us all out if we don't sit down and finish this game like gentlemen."

"That, sir, I deem impossible in the case of your brother," Strickland spat angrily. He was shaking, his fists clenching and unclenching.

Reede sat stoically contemplating his cards. He took an almost ladylike sip of his drink.

Pearce and Brawley, who were sitting between Strickland and Ben Macklowe, looked at each other, mute, not knowing what they were expected to do. Pearce was the larger of the two with a big red face and clipped blond hair. Brawley had some Indian blood in him, dark skin, black eyes, and thick black hair. Of the two, Brawley possessed more skill with horses and cows and was the quieter. Pearce flushed and flexed his arms, ready and willing to damage Reede Macklowe if that's what Strickland wanted. He only awaited word from the boss.

"Gentlemen, shall we stop this childishness and continue?" Ben Macklowe tried a gentle tone, hoping to soothe Strickland's intense anger—and to finish the game that had put him two hundred twenty dollars ahead. He needed the money.

Strickland sat down, steaming. He folded; Rettiger and Reede raised the stakes by another twenty dollars apiece; Macklowe, Pearce, and Brawley dropped out.

Rettiger's four tens beat Reede's four deuces, and he collected the pot.

Reede had finished his bottle and tossed back a long shot of his brother's Tennessee whiskey. He wiped his brow with the back of his hand. "I'll get it all back this time. My deal." He held out his hand to Brawley, who had dealt previously. He was not happy.

Strickland reached across the table and took the deck of cards from Brawley. He slammed the pasteboards onto the table. "We're through. You gentlemen will excuse us. Boys?" He pushed his chair back from the table and waited for Pearce and Brawley to do the same.

"Wait just a goddamned minute," Reede interjected.

"Reede," Macklowe said. He raised his hand to ask his brother to calm down.

But Reede Macklowe was having none of it. He would not quit on a losing hand. He'd sit there until noon if he had to to win just one more.

"No way these sheep dippers are going to walk out now before we finish cleaning them good."

Rettiger said, "It's a free country, Reede. We have been at this game a long time as it is. All night, in point of fact."

"It's a fact that these boys still have a few dollars in their pockets and I mean to relieve them of those dollars," Reede went on, unwilling to listen to Rettiger's or anyone else's words of common sense. "Strickland didn't spend everything at Julia's house. The girls there don't like to take his money, anyhow. They say he makes them do strange things, not like normal people."

Strickland tensed. He was a handsome fellow of about forty-five, with iron-gray hair and long sideburns and a jet black mustache. He wore his shirt open and collarless beneath a buckskin jacket that had seen many miles on the cow trails from Texas to Montana. Beneath the jacket he wore a blue-black Colt's Navy model .44-caliber revolver in a shoulder rig. He was tall and thin and badly in need of a shave—like the others assembled at the table. His thin black eyebrows twitched.

He moved around the table toward Reede. Ben Macklowe stepped between the two men. Strickland had six inches at least on Ben.

"That son of a bitch has gone too far. Get out of my way, Mr. Deputy Sheriff."

"Calm down, Mr. Strickland. Reede's trying to get your goat. Let's call it off and go to sleep—all of us."

Strickland stepped forward, bumping Macklowe, who took a step backward. In the cigar-smoke haze the men around the table tensed. At the far end of the lobby a clerk at the desk watched silently, prepared to run for the manager when and if any guns were brought into play.

"Let him come, Ben," Reede Macklowe said.

"Shut the hell up," Ben said. He kept himself between his brother and the angry Strickland.

Hinton Rettiger watched the two trail hands. He was not armed and they were. If it came to shooting, his only choice was to dive under the table, but he wanted to warn the deputy sheriff if the two raised their weapons outside Macklowe's vision. He sat with his big hands gripping the edge of the table.

"I will deal with you, too, if that is what you want," Strickland said to Ben Macklowe. His breath stank with whiskey and coffee.

Macklowe, whose own mouth was sour from the long night, said, "Neither you nor I want that, Mr. Strickland."

"Don't tell me what the hell I want, lawman."

"I just want to keep the peace here."

"Then lock up that piss-mouth brother of yours."

"Move back, Mr. Strickland," Ben said.

"Get out of my way," he replied, and took another unsteady step forward. His eyes burned whiskey mad.

"Go sleep it off," Ben insisted, standing his ground.

"You yellow, rodent-livered—" John Strickland swung his open hand, striking Ben Macklowe across the left cheek. The slap echoed through the room.

A hotel guest happened to be descending the staircase and stopped, turned, and went back upstairs.

Ben Macklowe touched the burning side of his face. He controlled the violent flare of temper that he felt in his brain. He would not let this situation become a full-fledged conflagration.

He said quietly, "Go to your room and sleep it off, Mr. Strickland."

Strickland was shocked at his own outburst and Macklowe's soft reaction. He was not quite certain he had actually done what he had done, and his anger intensified.

Brawley and Pearce sat there with their mouths open, and they did not move a muscle. Rettiger likewise was paralyzed with fear and amazement at Macklowe's absolutely cold response.

Only Reede was enjoying the whole scene. "You're a dead man, Strickland," he announced, shattering the glass wall of silence that had descended upon them all.

"You will regret those words," Strickland said. "I will take you down in a fair fight, and you will not know what hit you."

Strickland's shoulders slumped, his face flushed scarlet. He did not know what the hell to do now. He looked over to the two trail hands. "You boys go home, go to bed. I'll talk to you later." Then he spun around and walked heavily out of the lobby.

"Good night, Mr. Cowman!" Reede Macklowe shouted gaily after him.

"You say another word, I'll put you away for good," Ben said to his brother, anger surging within him almost beyond his control. He was sick of Reede's bullshit and he meant every word of it.

To Pearce and Brawley, the deputy sheriff said, "You men do what Mr. Strickland said. No hard feelings, just get the hell out of here. Now."

The two were gone like shadows in the glare of sunlight. That left Rettiger and the Macklowe brothers.

The newspaperman said, "This is front-page stuff, Ben. I've already written the headline: UGLY WORDS TRADED AT GRAND HOTEL GAMING FEUD. You are a wonder of self-control. I would have killed him if I had been you—or tried to."

"No sense in killing. He brings a lot of business to Saint Mary. Whitelaw and the town council would have my neck, even if it was provoked. I can't go around killing everybody who insults me."

"For God's sake the son of a bitch slapped your goddamned face!" Reede came over to his brother. "He was trying to start a riot. He wanted some killing."

"And I didn't give it to him," Ben said angrily. "No thanks to your mouth. I swear to God, Reede, you're out of control."

"Fellow can't take a joke," Reede muttered.

"You need to sleep it off." Ben turned away from him in disgust. "Want some breakfast, Hinton?"

"I'll buy," Rettiger said. He and Macklowe left Reede standing there with a stupid look on his face.

"Damn fools," the elder Macklowe said when they were gone. "They don't know what trouble is."

WHEN MACKLOWE REPORTED TO THE OFFICE FOR THE night shift, Whitelaw was there waiting for him.

"How many times have I told you to stay away from the damn card games, Ben?"

"If you paid me better, I might not need to make a little on the side."

"The county pays our salary and the town council tolerates us—reluctantly. You want to be rich, you're in the wrong place, Major."

"War's over, Claude. Stop calling me that."

"Can't help it. Sometimes it comes out. You're a natural leader, Ben. I couldn't have stood up to Strickland like that without shooting a hole in his goddamned forehead and getting my own guts blown out. But you shouldn't have been in that position in the first place. And your brother—"

"I've heard enough from you and everybody else about Reede." He stuffed his hands in his pocket.

"And you'll be hearing plenty more until he gets the hell out of Saint Mary."

"I'm working on that."

"The man has no human sympathy for that poor girl who died because of him, he can't stop drinking even though he gets in trouble every time he picks up a bottle, he almost gets his own brother killed for no good reason other than his foul mouth." Whitelaw took off his sweat-stained hat and slammed it on the desk.

"If you want my resignation, you can have it."

"No way in hell is that what I want and you know it. You're talking crazy. What I want is peace in this town, and I want you to go to Strickland and talk to him on the quiet and straighten this thing out. I don't want any gun challenges and showdowns or any of that bullshit in my county. I get paid to prevent that from happening, and I pay you to help me. So go do it."

Ben Macklowe stopped by Jain's shop before he went to see Strickland. He told her what had happened.

She kissed him. "I missed you last night," was all she said. She had her way of making him feel guilty about things like that.

He said, "My poker-playing days are numbered, anyhow. I've got enough of a stake put away to buy a piece of land outside of town here, maybe start a cow spread of my own. Good place to raise up a kid."

Her eyes lit up. "What if it's a little girl?"

"I'll be happy if it's a two-headed goat."

"Stop talking like that!" She threw someone's soiled shirt at him. "Get out of here."

"I'm long gone," he said, then stopped in the door. "I get off tonight at six. Dinner?"

"Maybe," she said.

CHAPTER 6

JOHN STRICKLAND HAD A SUITE AT THE STOCKMEN'S CLUB
on Third Street. It was not an opulent place, but offered
cleanliness and plenty of comfort. Downstairs was a res-
taurant that served good hot food, a bar, a sitting room
with high-backed chairs, and a meeting room in back for
serious cow business. Upstairs were six sleeping rooms
and two larger suites for overnight guests. Saint Mary saw
its share of traveling cattle folk, and in the heyday of the
trail drives they used to come through in big numbers.
Used to be the stock pens near the railroad station were not
big enough to accommodate some of the herds that were
quartered in town before the last leg of the trip to Montana.
And some of the cattlemen liked what they saw here in
Absaroka County and decided to stay, buy up some of the
rich foothill country, and open their own outfits.

The McTiernans were the biggest and oldest cattle family in the county, and they were the chief sellers to cattle
buyers like Strickland. The McTiernan clan went back to
the days before the Rebellion; they were the first white
people besides the old trappers to make this country their
home and to fight off anybody—red or white—who chal-
lenged their right to do so.

Old Jack McTiernan—he was in his late seventies now
—had two sons, David and Patrick, who kept the business
running profitably. There were now three houses on the Big
T ranch, the father's and the two sons'. A new generation

45

was coming up: David had two boys, Patrick had three daughters.

For the most part, the McTiernans were benign monarchs who had little truck with townfolk from Saint Mary. Other than the political honchos and the Catholic priest who lived in a neat McTiernan-built rectory next to the parish church, there were few citizens who had any contact at all with the family.

A fellow like John Strickland saw the two McTiernan sons once or twice a year, did his business, pocketed his commission, and moved on. Strickland was more or less a broker for an Omaha outfit, and he spent a lot of time in hotel rooms in Wyoming and Montana.

Macklowe went straight to his room and knocked, waited at the door.

It took a few minutes for Strickland to respond, trying Macklowe's patience. When the door opened, the occupant of the room was not pleased to see his visitor.

"What do you want?" His long, lean face looked gray and sapped of life. The all-night game had depleted him.

"To talk. Sheriff Whitelaw wants to keep the peace, doesn't want you or your boys walking around mad."

"I have no quarrel with Whitelaw. Your brother is a different story. But I don't intend to seek him out—it's not worth the trouble. By the way, I'm sorry I hit you."

Macklowe had not expected the apology. For a second he was at a loss for anything to say. Then he managed, "I will not hold it against you. Reede can be rilesome at times." He held out his hand.

Strickland took it, gave it a firm shake. "Want to come in for a drink?"

Ben Macklowe knew he drank too much, not as much as his brother, but still too much. Yet to turn down an offer for a free drink went against his very nature. He accepted Strickland's invitation without a second thought. A drink or two wouldn't hurt, in fact might help keep him moving on a day that had started out bad.

Macklowe seated himself on a chintz-covered sofa facing a brace of windows that opened onto the street. The sun shone through the dirty panes and a breeze rattled them a bit. It was warm and secure in here. It smelled of temporary living, a man used to sleeping in strange places. He lit up a cigarette and watched Strickland pour whiskey into a tall tumbler. He filled it about halfway and gave it to Ben.

Strickland sat in a straight chair and crossed his legs. His buckskin jacket was thrown across the bed, and a valise lay open at the foot of the bed, with clothing stuffed into it haphazardly. Strickland took a sip from his drink and watched Macklowe looking around the room and tried to see it—and himself—as Macklowe saw it.

"I won't be here for more than a couple of days," he said to Macklowe. "I have business up in Billings, then I'm going hunting in December."

"Hunting for sport?" Macklowe regarded Strickland with a jaundiced eye. He could not fathom using firearms for mere sport—not when he had seen so much use of them in war and in law work.

Strickland said, "Some gentlemen from the East will be wintering at a lodge on the Little Missouri. They want to go out on 'safari.' I'm taking them—for money."

"There must be an easier way to make money."

"Plenty of easier ways, but not as much money. These dudes are willing to pay a high premium for a taste of the Wild West."

Macklowe thought back on his own career as a soldier in two armies, a gambler, a lawman, a wanderer. He thought about his wife in Austin, about the women he had known. What would John Strickland's "dudes" make of him: a real specimen of the Wild West, he supposed, born in Canada and raised up in Texas, more comfortable with a pistol in his hand than not.

Strickland poured two more drinks. "My employers are out of Omaha; it's an up-and-coming town. You ever thought of going into the cattle business?"

"Not sober." Macklowe raised his glass.

* * *

REEDE WAS DRINKING AS WELL. HE HAD NO PLACE TO STAY, so he found a tavern that opened early—it really never closed its doors—and he made it his home base. The saloon keeper brought him a bottle of warm beer and Reede took a wobbly table in a dark corner. There was no one else there until two men came in about an hour later: Strickland's riders, Pearce and Brawley. At first they did not see Reede Macklowe, and he made no effort to show himself. Then Pearce, the skinnier of the two, with his face stove in beneath his cheekbones, turned away from the bar and discerned the outline of a man in the corner. He elbowed his partner. Brawley saw Reede then, too.

"The son of a bitch is following us around," Brawley muttered.

"How could he? He came in here before we did." Sometimes the depth of Brawley's stupidity baffled his riding partner.

The two had stopped by Miss Julia's house and done their business and now sought to get a little drunker before hitting their bedrolls outside of town. They could not afford a hotel room.

Reede watched them with apparently little interest, as if they were a pair of performing dogs in a traveling show. They were certainly less attractive than their canine brethren.

He was very drunk by now: sit-down, slit-eyed drunk. He barely possessed the power to lift his glass to his lips, but he was not finished drinking. He would put the stuff down his throat until he passed out. His brain, however, functioned beautifully.

Brawley called over to him, "Those whores are talking about you, Macklowe. Say you're a real mean lover man. One little girl hung herself for pining after you."

Reede Macklowe did not move from his chair, but he tensed almost imperceptibly. His grip tightened around the empty glass on the table.

Pearce said to his companion, "He loved her to death is what he done—ha!" The cowboys clinked their glasses and drank. Pearce went on, "I wonder how many men, women, and children that's happened to."

"And how many sheep and cows," Brawley added.

The taunts did not penetrate the red-hot core of Reede's anger. He was already angry before these emaciated hired boys arrived—angry at his brother, at Saint Mary, at the world. These two were a sideshow. In his alcohol-inflamed mind he was beginning to formulate an idea . . . an idea of how to get back at all of the sons of bitches—or else to exit the world with a bullet in his own gut and take some of them with him.

Pearce and Brawley, thinking their taunts were having no effect, tried harder and louder for several minutes. Reede remained unmoved and unmoving. Finally their crude jokes tapered off and they started to concentrate more on their drinking. They turned their backs to Reede and therefore did not see him several minutes later coming toward them, bottle in hand.

With a sudden movement he slammed the empty whiskey bottle onto the rough bar at Brawley's elbow. The two cowboys jumped a foot and reached for their belt guns. Reede, however, held a revolver to Brawley's ear—in fact poked into his ear with the end of the cold barrel.

"You gentlemen care for another drink? Or do you have other business to attend to?"

"Pearce, don't make a goddamn move, he's got a gun in my ear," Brawley said.

Thad Pearce holstered his pistol, as did Brawley. Then Pearce said, "You hurt my friend and I'll blow a hole in your head so wide they can drive a pregnant cow through it."

"Don't try to be clever, dust-eater, it doesn't become you," Reede said. "If I decide to kill your boyfriend, nobody's going to persuade me not to. Especially you."

"Pearce, just be quiet," Brawley said through yellow clenched teeth. Sweat poured down his temples.

"Now, what were you saying about that poor girl? My brother told me how she killed herself. It almost made me cry. I said almost. Don't you think it's sad? Don't you, woolly lover?" Reede poked the gun barrel farther into the man's ear, catching the sight on the tender flesh there.

Brawley winced and tried to pull away, but Reede held his right arm firmly and did not allow him to move.

The barkeep stood at the far end of the room, watching. There was no one else on the premises, so this little melodrama was acted before an audience of one. The tavern was dark and musty smelling; you wouldn't know there was a bright cold November day in full bloom outside.

Reede Macklowe removed the revolver from Brawley's ear and put it on the bar. He unbuckled his gun belt and placed it atop the revolver. He took a step back.

"You two are real tough with the mouth. Let's see if you can back it up. Which one wants to take me first?"

Brawley spun away from Reede, bumping into his friend as he tried to put some space between himself and his attacker. Pearce caught Brawley and steadied him. Pearce was usually the more levelheaded of the pair, but he was seeing red now. He held his Smith & Wesson .32-caliber rimfire five-shot First Issue, his palm sweating on the rosewood grips.

"I'm obliged to kill you, Mr. Macklowe," he said.

Reede stood erect and smiled insouciantly. "You talk pretty for a cowchaser, son. Real nice and polite. Listen, there's going to be no killing here—but I want to teach you and your friend a lesson. Put that goddamned popgun down and fight like a two-legged man."

Brawley, who had not stopped shaking, looked to his riding partner. "Shoot him," he hissed.

Reede did not take his eyes off Pearce and the little five-shooter. Brawley was a distraction. He said to Pearce, "Make up your mind. Shoot like a coward or stand and fight. The day grows short."

Pearce was not a bad or dishonest man, but he had no anchor in his life: no mother, no wife or girlfriend, no child, no home, no permanent job. The only constant in his young life to date had been Ned Brawley, friend and trail partner. It seemed that when Ned got drunk, Thad Pearce got drunk, too. When Ned got into a fight, Thad Pearce got into a fight, too. When Ned opened his mouth, so did Pearce.

Now, Pearce was in the position of defending his friend's and his own "honor" by taking on this drunken stranger who had turned a simple poker game into a war the previous night. Macklowe was taller but softer around the middle. Pearce was a bantam-feisty one hundred fifteen pounds with a solid torso that could take a lot of punishment—and had in times past.

He carefully holstered his Smith & Wesson, unbuckled the gun belt, and handed the rig to Brawley.

"You're a crazy fool, Thad," Brawley said.

"Not crazy, just mad," Pearce replied. He was also more than a bit drunk and dog-tired. All he really wanted to do was find someplace to put his bedroll and sleep.

Reede Macklowe watched every movement, remembering times when he and his brother had been in just this predicament—or worse. He was not even sure why he wanted to pick a fight with these two: their insults and taunts about the girl were not the real reason. He shifted his trousers to give himself some freedom of motion, rolled up his sleeves. These were automatic responses, unconsciously executed. His eyes bored in on Pearce.

He said, "What's it going to be?"

Pearce said to Brawley, "If either one of us gets hurt, you fetch a doctor." He glanced over to the tavern owner, who stood in the shadows, silent.

Brawley said, "You're gonna flatten him, Thad."

"Shall we stop talking, gentlemen, and start fighting?"

Pearce stepped up. He was a full head shorter than Reede Macklowe but seemingly quicker on his feet. He bounced upon the balls of his feet, lifted his gnarled fists. Macklowe saw the hair on Pearce's knuckles.

Brawley stepped back, dropped the gun belt on the bar, and began biting his nails. "Get him," he muttered.

Pearce threw the first punch: a right aimed at Reede's

jaw. Reede blocked it with his right forearm.

Reede was somewhat surprised at the power behind the blow. He rocked back on his right foot and came forward with his own right, connecting with Pearce's cheekbone and breaking skin. Pearce staggered back, dabbed his face with the back of his fist, which came away bloody.

Quickly, he undercut the taller man's arms and planted a left, then a right in Reede's unprotected gut.

The air whooshed out of Reede Macklowe's lungs and he doubled over, trying at the same time to step backward, but Pearce moved in and battered his face with a jab and a stinging right.

Reede staggered back, warding off a flurry from Pearce, trying desperately to regain his balance. He performed a demented dance until he finally found his footing and was able to right himself. Then he charged at the smaller man.

Pearce stood his ground, raised his arms defensively, took several body blows. Now he stepped backward, but he could not escape Reede's onslaught. Macklowe swung mightily—right, left, right, left—and Pearce gamely took the punishment as much as he ducked and weaved.

Reede stopped to catch his breath, kept his distance from the constantly bobbing cowboy. His dark hair hung in his eyes and perspiration poured down his face; beneath his shirt his body was soaked.

Seeing an opportunity, Pearce took a half step forward and delivered a mean left uppercut that caught Reede squarely beneath his chin. It shut Reede's mouth with a crunch, and blood trickled from each end of his lips.

Reede shook his dark head, spraying blood over his opponent. He tried to speak, but his mouth felt liquid and several teeth were loose.

"Good shot, Thad!" Brawley called.

Pearce turned for a split second to acknowledge his friend's cheer and turned back in time to see Macklowe's big right fist in his face. The fist crashed into Pearce's left eye, stunning him. His hands went up to his face.

Reede pummeled the cowboy's ribs, cracking a couple,

then kneed him in the groin. Pearce buckled. Reede raised his coupled hands to stun the broken son of a bitch.

A shot rang out and wood chips and splinters showered the fighters. Pearce hit his knees. Reede swung around the bar and ducked.

Brawley shot Pearce's Smith & Wesson again and again. Pearce was on the floor, beyond hearing or caring. He moaned lightly.

Reede Macklowe came out from behind the bar. "You stupid ass," he said.

The barkeep was nowhere to be seen. Brawley bent over his friend.

"You and your brother are going to be dead before the day ends," Brawley said.

Reede spat out blood and teeth. He poured himself a glass of whiskey, took some, and spat that out, too. He said, "You name the time and the place."

"Four o'clock, on American Street. You and your brother."

"And who will you bring to protect your ass?"

Brawley did not respond. Reede replaced his gun belt and went to the door. He called back to Brawley and Pearce, "See you later, gents."

CHAPTER 7

BEN MACKLOWE WAS TRYING TO SLEEP. JAIN WORKED
next door, bent over the steaming laundry vats. Macklowe,
fully dressed, except for his boots, opened his eyes and
stared at the ceiling of Jain's bedroom, his breath ragged
from too much smoking, his brain soggy from too much
booze.

He had a terrific headache.

He could not get the girl's suicide out of his mind, and
he kept remembering the half-crazy Mormon prophet who
had been preaching on the cold street that night, probably
at the same time the girl was killing herself. It bothered
him. Macklowe had no prejudice against religion, although
he personally hated it, but he did not hate any man for his
religion.

He had had his run-in with a Mormon renegade a few
years ago, during his drifting days. It came back to him in
a rush of images. He closed his eyes again, tried again to
sleep, but instead began to relive a day from the recent
past, before he had even heard of Saint Mary, Wyoming
Territory. . . .

EASY MONEY STOP LOTS OF IT STOP YOU KNOW WHERE I
AM STOP SIGNED JOE JARGONE

That's what the telegraph said when it caught up to
Macklowe in El Paso where he was doing fine at the tables
—a hundred dollars a day's worth, give or take a few bits

54

—and not so bad in the female department. It was late spring, that bitching time of year when it's hot as hell in the day and cold as a rich man's wife at night.

Macklowe left the border town for Salt Lake City. It took a week to get out of New Mexico and another several days to reach the Wasatch Range. His horse, a smooth-tempered stallion, missed the regular El Paso meals as much as Macklowe did, so the rider didn't push him hard.

At noon Macklowe was well up into the mountains, looking out on some of the most beautiful and deadly country God had scooped out of the clay. He had just cleared a giant boulder on the narrow trail that snaked up the east face of the peak and was feeling mightily grateful that mount and rider had not fallen into the gorge below when a bullet screamed past his face.

Then another gun opened up and lead spanged off the rock behind him. His horse whickered in fear, but Macklowe calmed him and managed to dodge around another boulder that lay beneath a craggy ledge.

He dismounted as more shooting exploded above his head. He could not tell for sure how many men there were —but no doubt too many for his liking.

Quickly he unsheathed his big Winchester .44-40 and pushed the horse along out of the way. It would be pretty inconvenient—if he didn't get killed—to lose his mount and have to walk the rest of the way.

Macklowe opened fire from a handy cleft between the rock and the mountain, aiming for the blue smoke that hazed around an outcropping above him and to his right. That got an answer. He held off and tried to count the guns. Sounded like there were a pair, but again, he could not be certain.

Who the hell is out there shooting at me? he wondered. He threw a few more bullets at them, chipping rock in their faces. When he was finished, he had spent half of the sixteen shots in his rifle. The unseen bushwhackers kept firing as Macklowe considered that the odds, at two to one, weren't that bad.

For a while Macklowe sat quiet and waited—waited for one of them to get smart and figure maybe they had shot him. It didn't take long.

One of them ordered the other to cease fire. Macklowe took off his hat and slid back to the notch in the rock and aimed for the patch of sky along the ridgeline where they were. He could hear them talking between themselves, and then a head appeared in that patch of sky.

He put a single shot through the bushwhacker's forehead. The man toppled from the rock without a sound, his gun clattering down after him. That spooked the other. He stood and started spitting lead at Macklowe like he was the angry Jehovah raining fire and brimstone over those sinners in Sodom and Gomorrah. Bullets spanged all around Macklowe, but he remained unhurt. Then the man howled like a mad dog. More lead followed.

After letting him spend a few more bullets, Macklowe took aim and blasted him off the ridge.

The hit in the arm sent him spinning backward with a scream of fear. Macklowe crept from behind the big rock back along the trail until he came to a spot where he could climb up toward the ridge where the wounded man lay— cursing him, ready to kill him. Quiet as he tried to be, Macklowe's boots scraped loudly on the bare rock.

"One step more and I'll shoot!" came the agonized shout from behind the craggy outcropping just ten yards from where Macklowe crouched.

Macklowe picked up a ten-pound rock, heaved it down over the trail, and hollered. That brought the wounded bushwhacker up again and Macklowe clipped his good arm with another shot. He fell back and Macklowe moved over the ridge with his Winchester ready to blow the fool's head off if he again tried to play tough.

He did. He was waiting for his target with his belt gun, a Smith & Wesson .38, in a bloody fist, barely able to lift his shattered arm to discharge it.

"Put it down, or you are a dead man," Macklowe said.

The gunman dropped the revolver and begged Macklowe with his eyes not to kill him. He was a young fellow and wore a blue felt hat.

Macklowe went down and disarmed him, taking up his revolver, his rifle, a sharp clean hunting knife, and—patting him down beneath his coat—a headaway gun tucked into a vest pocket. He threw the weapons over the side of the mountain where they would be of no use to anyone anymore, let alone this bloodied cayuse.

"Lie easy, friend." Macklowe didn't need to say it. The bushwhacker didn't move as Macklowe went back to his horse and tied the animal to a gnarled root in the side of the mountain and took his saddlebag back to the bushwhacker's campsite.

Macklowe built a fire with a few dry sticks kindly provided by the would-be killers. There were a lot of questions he wanted to ask the wounded man, but he took his time with the fire.

When the flame was burning well, Macklowe retrieved a bottle of whiskey from his saddlebag and uncorked it and took a big slug. It burned through right to his gut, felt good. Then he turned to the blue-hatted, bullet-shot man who lay bleeding beside him.

"Drink?" he offered.

The cayuse's eyes bulged out of his pale face. He was hurt bad, had lost a lot of blood already. Macklowe wondered if the liquor might not be the best thing in the world for him—but he seemed to think it was. He nodded like a panhandler at a sympathetic mark. Macklowe held out the bottle to him, then drew it back. He took another swallow and smacked his lips loudly and declared that it was the best whiskey he'd had in a long time.

"Please," the man croaked.

"Say 'pretty please' when you are talking to me."

The bushwhacker did not see the humor in Macklowe's joke. The poor bastard was at the end of the rope and all he wanted was a drink. Macklowe was feeling mean enough to hold out on him, but if he wanted the asshole to talk, he'd have to loosen his tongue.

"One swallow," Macklowe told him.

It was the biggest swallow he had ever taken in his life. The whiskey ran over his face and down his chin like he was taking a bath in it. Macklowe let him drink. His Adam's apple pistoned up and down. Finally Macklowe pulled the bottle away.

"Say thank you."

It took a while for the whiskey to trickle down the man's throat and he swallowed a few times before he rasped, "Thank you."

"Your mother taught you good manners, son. I hear she once took on a whole regiment of Yankee soldiers. Must be you got some military blood in you, some polite and proper ancestors." The man moved his mouth but nothing came out. "No, I'm serious—for the son of a pockmarked whore you turned out all right." Macklowe put aside thoughts of his own questionable parentage as he said, "What would she say if she could see the mess you are in now?"

"Don't kill me, mister. Please." Sweat ran down his eyes mixing with the tears.

"You are a quick learner," Macklowe said. "Hope your sweet mother also taught you to tell the truth. You know, I always say there is nothing lower than a dirty low-down liar."

"Sure thing, mister."

"Here, have another drink. On the house." Macklowe touched the bottle to the man's teeth before he yanked it away once more. "Talk," he said. "Who told you to kill me?"

"Nobody did, honest. Brad and me, we just—"

Macklowe slapped him across the face and felt his nose break under his palm and heard bone and cartilage crack. Blood spread over the bushwhacker's face and ran into his mouth. Macklowe lifted his head and he spat and coughed and gagged like he had consumption.

"That's not the way it is done, friend," Macklowe said. "Talk straight or don't talk at all. One more lie from that mouth of yours and you can forget about ever waking up again. Who hired you to kill me?"

The man said again that it was just his buddy Brad and himself who thought up the idea of skinning the rider on the mountainside.

Macklowe backhanded him and put his nose on the other side of his face, and he howled like a whipped pup.

Macklowe sat back and took another pull on the bottle. Then he rolled a cigarette and smoked it until the man quieted down.

"You hungry?" Macklowe asked him.

He didn't answer, so Macklowe popped open a 'tin of peaches and ate them with his knife and drank the sweet sticky juice. He wasn't really that hungry, but he wanted to remind the other what he was missing in the world. Another swallow of whiskey washed the peach taste from his mouth and he asked again, "Who hired you?"

"Like I said—"

Up on his feet, the Winchester cocked, Macklowe aimed the long barrel at the bushwhacker's chest.

"Your time is up, boy. You have got three seconds to give me what I want or you are a dead man. One . . . two . . ."

"I'll talk! I'll talk!"

Macklowe carefully levered the rifle's hammer down.

"Brad and me, we took our orders from a man named Mr. Abraham. Never saw his face, not once. I swear to God I don't know who he is. Only met him once—at night and he wore a mask. You got to believe me, mister! I'm telling you the God's truth now."

"Talk to me."

It was hard to hear what he said through the blood and all his sobbing. He knew by this time that he was a goner; his chest heaved with every word as he spilled his story.

"I—I told Brad we shouldn't do it. I didn't like the whole idea."

"I can see why," Macklowe said. "Describe this Mr.

59

Abraham character to me. Tall? Short? Old man? What did he talk like?"

The young man's entire life seemed to pass before his eyes. He was in his early twenties, Macklowe gauged. Hadn't lived very much of life yet, so there couldn't be a hell of a lot to regret. His voice faded. He had bled badly, but Macklowe did not lift a finger to stanch the wounds.

The bushwhacker breathed hard and long. "Tall . . ." He closed his eyes. "I can see him now—tall—and he's kind of skinny—and—"

"Have another drink." Macklowe lifted his head to pour the whiskey down his throat. The man swallowed some, but more dripped from the sides of his mouth.

"What else?"

"It's dark," the youth moaned. "Brad—where are you, Brad?"

"Your buddy Brad is dead, my friend. Tell me more about this Mr. Abraham."

"Don't know nothing . . ." he wheezed. The sticky red stuff bubbled out of his mouth.

Then his face went white as chalk; he didn't have much blood left in him. His lips moved but no words came out. He was trying to tell Macklowe to believe him. He wanted to die with a clean conscience.

Macklowe put a slug through his skull to take him out of his misery. It got very quiet on the mountain after the young bushwhacker gave up the ghost. Macklowe went through his pockets. He found a letter addressed to Sam Rodgers. So that was the corpse's handle. That's all he found, other than five dollars, which he pocketed for miscellaneous damages. Macklowe picked up Sam Rodgers and tossed him over the precipice to join his shooting partner Brad in a deep grave no one but the buzzards and the mountain cats would ever disturb.

It was nearing sunset by that time, so Macklowe decided to make camp right there. He fetched his horse around to where the bushwhackers' animals were tethered. He was now richer by two horses and five dollars—more than he'd expected when he woke up that morning. Still, it made him uncomfortable to think he had taken this bounty from two men who had tried to kill him.

He hunkered down to tend the fire, sipping on that good whiskey, as the sun sank behind the big bulking mountains above him. He let the red coals burn down some before he fried two slices of slab bacon on a rock and mixed the meat with a can of red beans. That and the whiskey filled him sufficiently.

He watered and fed the horses, then relaxed by the fire with a cigarette. He leaned back against a rounded rock and looked up at the sky as a quarter moon and the stars came out.

Times like that Macklowe did his best thinking.

The more he thought about him, the less he liked this mysterious Mr. Abraham. Not only because he wanted Macklowe dead, but because he chose a couple of greenhorns to do the job. Showed he had no respect for Macklowe and no guts himself.

Macklowe was not very flexible in such matters, for he was convinced that there was a right way and a wrong way to do anything.

CHAPTER 8

MACKLOWE STIRRED UNCOMFORTABLY, GUNFIRE ECHOING in his mind, an adumbration of trouble, a pain in his gut. Joe Jargone was long dead now. The mysterious Mr. Abraham had been a two-bit empire builder who didn't want anyone of Macklowe's caliber anywhere near his field of operation and hadn't been willing to pay for top-quality muscle to keep Macklowe at bay.

None of it had paid off: the gambling, the gunplay, the smart words, the quick scores.

For the first time in his life, Ben Macklowe had begun to feel at home, comfortable in his own boots, since he took this job with Whitelaw and met Jain Dobbie. It was all working out just fine until Reede came back. That boy was trouble, and he didn't give a good goddamn who knew it.

Macklowe's mind was confused: for a moment he could not remember if Reede was a boy or a man or simply a figure from his own imagination that sometimes was real, sometimes not. The drinking was getting out of hand. Jain had said something to him the other day. He saw it in Reede, too—maybe more than himself.

Perhaps he should leave Saint Mary, give up the pretense of legitimacy. God bless Claude Whitelaw, but he could not make an honest man of Ben Macklowe, try as he might. But where would he go if he threw all this over?

Was there any better hope of making a new start else-where?

Sweat beaded his forehead. He brushed back his thin-ning hair. When he had freed Reede from prison and told him about the girl who had committed suicide, Reede had for just a moment reacted as Ben had hoped he would.

"Dead?" he had said. His blue eyes clouded. "Did she leave a letter—anything?"

"Julia destroyed it."

"That bitch."

"She probably thought she was doing the best thing."

"Don't give her more credit than she's due, Ben. She would as soon skin a dog as eat it. I never liked her much with her painted face and tarty dresses and red hair."

"She never liked you much, either."

"Julia can go to hell for all I care—and she will."

Then Ben had changed the subject. "Why did you come back, anyway, Reede? You left some angry people here from your last visit."

"I know, brother. Came down to nowhere else to go. I bought a horse down in Texas and pointed it in this direc-tion. Took my time. The old nag won't be much good for anybody else. Livery might want to rent her out to pull some old lady's buggy."

"Doesn't come close to answering my question."

"You ask too many questions. Always have."

"Reede, what the hell are you doing with your life? Every time you get drunk you get into trouble. You leave Saint Mary with half the town mad at you—the other half mad at me. If Whitelaw weren't such a decent chap, he'd have told me to go with you. Now you come back—drunk and disorderly—no explanation, no money, no prospects. You're in seriously bad shape and I want to help you but you won't let me."

"Always the good Christian brother."

"It's not that and you know it. I can't claim to have my life in order, but I'm giving it a try. I want something better than what I've had—which is nothing."

"Well, you go to it, brother. You can get what you want, but it's not what I want."

"What do you want?"

"Oh, maybe a nice-looking colored girl like you have." He stretched his lips in an infuriating grin. "Now, don't be offended. I'm just jealous is all."

Ben Macklowe turned over in bed, rehearsing the conversation with his brother several times in his head.

It melded into other conversations, other events, other times. When he had been a federal prisoner of war, then served as a colonel in Maximilian's imperial army after the War Between the Sates, he had lost track of Reede.

The brothers had been reunited in El Paso, quite by accident one day about nine years ago. They had sat down at the same gaming table—directly across from each other—and played for two hours, each a winner, before leaving the game and the house together to embrace and try to catch up on the lost years and drink each other under the table at a series of saloons that got darker and dingier as the night progressed. . . .

Ben swung his feet around and lit a ready-made cigarette, violently pulling the smoke into his lungs. It was well past noon by now. He had given Reede permission to stay at his place. As if Reede needed permission to do anything he damn well pleased. Macklowe almost smiled at the thought of his brother's pigheadedness. The smoke went to his head and made him pleasantly dizzy. He needed a drink, but knew Jain would be intensely displeased if he were to do so without any sleep or any food in his stomach.

He heard her singing now: a soft, low voice, sweet in its spiritual intensity. She was a special woman, and he often wondered why she put up with his drinking and his black moods. Suddenly the singing stopped. He heard a man's voice, then Jain's in reply.

Macklowe knew before he went out of the bedroom who it was. Reede stood in the front door, or rather held himself up at the front door, a battered, shadowed wreck of a man.

He reeked of liquor—even Macklowe could smell it all the way across the room.

"Got a bathtub?" Reede asked, removing a bloodied hand from the doorjamb.

"This is not my house, Reede. I'm not the one to ask," Macklowe said with an edge of anger in his voice.

"She won't mind."

"Ask her," Macklowe said. He clenched his fists at his side, ready at any more provocation to finish the job someone had begun on his brother's face.

"All right." Reede stumbled out and went next door.

Ben Macklowe went to the pantry, removed a half-full bottle of Kentucky whiskey, poured himself a tall shot, and took it in a single swallow.

Reede returned with Jain's permission to use her tub, and she followed him and went to Ben. "I've got a ten-gallon vat of steaming water next door. You two gentlemen will carry it over here, please."

Ben helped Reede prepare the bath and watched as his brother stripped his torn and bloodied clothes off and stepped into the hot water. His drunkenness seemed to melt off and his skin took on a healthier color. Ben sat in a chair next to the tub.

"Are you going to tell me what the hell happened?"

"Well, I got into a fistfight with one of those cowboys that sided Strickland at the poker game. His name is Pearce, I think. The uglier of the two."

"I thought you were going to my room to sleep."

"Stopped for a drink at a dingy little cantina on the other side of this lovely town of yours."

"This drinking is going to kill you."

"Don't preach at me, brother. You drink enough for any ten men you care to name. It's part of our makeup, not anybody's fault."

"But you carry it too far, Reede. Tell me about this fight. You didn't start it, I assume."

"No, and damned near almost didn't finish it. The other one—the one who looks like a fairy—shot the shit out of

65

the ceiling and like to scare me to death." He laughed a huge, devilish laugh, his blue eyes sparking like flints. He cupped the soapy water and washed his face. "I was making pulp of his boyfriend—after Pearce had done a pretty good piece of work on me, I must say. Ouch!" He touched his swollen mouth.

"Any particular reason for the fisticuffs?"

"I guess we both just wanted an excuse to box someone around a bit. Seemed like the right thing to do at the time. We were both drunk."

"That much I knew already. How much damage did you do to the tavern?" Macklowe lit a fresh cigarette.

"You'll have to talk to the barkeep about that. Plenty to the ceiling, but we didn't bust up any chairs or tables or glass."

"What is it you are not telling me, Reede? I can see it in your bloodshot eyes."

"Well, Pearce wants to meet me at four o'clock on American Street across from the courthouse." He submerged himself in the hot, soapy water and reemerged to take a gulp of air into his aching lungs.

Ben Macklowe sat without moving, without speaking, waiting for his brother to finish.

Reede looked over at Ben, wiped the soapsuds from his brow. "Can I have a drag on that?" he asked.

Ben put the cigarette between Reede's lips. Reede breathed in the acrid smoke and sat back in the tub.

"You're invited, too," he said finally.

"I'm not surprised. I tell you what. I'll speak to Claude Whitelaw about all this. We'll call it off. I'm not going to be a party to more bloodshed in Saint Mary. And neither are you, you stupid, arrogant, drunken bum."

Jain Dobbie came in then, looking tired and beautiful, a wisp of black hair snaking from her high forehead over one eyebrow. She looked first at Ben, then at Reede Macklowe. It baffled her, the difference between these two men who were blood brothers—and the similarity.

"What are you two talking about that has made you so angry, Ben?"

"My brother's stupidity makes me angry. And his unconcern for a single human being other than himself. He's got us into some duel or other this afternoon."

"It's not as if we aren't going to win," Reede said.

"That is not the point. I am a deputy sheriff of this county, and I cannot become involved in your petty gambling feuds, brother." Macklowe was livid. He rose and stood in the front doorway. He was not tall, but he filled the light-strewn door and his anger was large, filling the very room.

"I have changed, Reede. I have tried to change. If it weren't for that old man, I don't know where the hell I would be. He has saved my life, given me something—I don't even know what the hell it is—" He slammed his fist against the open door in frustration.

"It's damned cold in here with that door wide open," Reede said.

Jain Dobbie brought Reede a big cotton towel, then turned away as he emerged from the bathtub and dried himself. She took away his torn and bloodied clothes to mend and clean and laid out a suit of Ben's for him.

She went over to Ben. "You want a cup of coffee?"

"Yes, please, darling," he said. He did not look at his brother. A thousand unpleasant and violent thoughts raced through his mind.

Reede said, "I haven't had a bath like that in nearly a year. Thanks, Miss Dobbie, it was kind of you."

"Least I can do for a dying man," she muttered.

"You two make a damned gloomy house, I'll say that much."

Ben said, "You've said a damn sight too much already. I suggest you shut your mouth for the duration, Reede."

OUTSIDE THE COURTHOUSE A FOUR-INCH FEDERAL CANNON, retired honorably from the wars, pointed due north with impotent menace. The children and birds of Saint Mary had long since plugged the rusted barrel with detritus.

Near the cannon, as the sun fell again behind the big shoulders of the mountains, a young man paced to and fro, speaking loudly. It was the prophet. He had returned to bring the gospel to the people of this less than God-fearing town. The descending chill had the opposite effect on him: it warmed him to his mission.

"My friends," he shouted to no one in particular, for there were few folks about. "We are God's children, created in his image and likeness with dominion over the Earth. This is the revealed truth of God and it is our bounden duty to live according to God's plan. What do we know, brothers and sisters, of God's mind? We know what is revealed in the Scriptures. We know what the church teaches. And it is the gravest of sins to know and not to act upon the will of the Almighty.

"Sinners we are, the lot of us, since we do not heed Him, do not call upon Him, do not serve Him. Yet He loves us still, despite the violence we do to His name."

The wind gusted, chilling the earth and blowing the young man's hat brim against the side of his head as he stood near the quiet cannon and preached.

A straw-haired woman holding a boy's hand walked toward the dark-coated prophet. She stopped about ten yards from him and listened as the boy fidgeted at her side, turning to look at the cannon instead of the man of God.

"We are charged to go among the nations and shout the good news of salvation to the heathen and the hard of heart. When will we listen to the Lord God of Hosts who bids us come unto Him to be saved, to live forever in peace, to follow His son who died for all mankind upon the cross. The promise of eternal life is no joke, brethren, but the very essence of God's love for His children. Here—in this book all His magnificent promises are written, His words to the Chosen People are recorded for us, the Chosen Ones of the latter days. For it was revealed unto the Prophet Joseph Smith that the Holy Church of God that had fallen away would be restored to the glory and honor of the

Almighty Father—and we are invited to sup at the table of the Lord in His Holy Church. We are called in these days of tribulation and sin to follow the Word, to love the Father and our neighbor, to succor the children and teach them the Word, to live as God has shown us through His only Son Jesus Christ."

The woman prodded her boy and they moved away. A golden light fell upon the prophet and the bell in the court-house clock tolled four.

CHAPTER 9

IN THE LATE AFTERNOON, BEFORE THE COURTHOUSE CLOCK tolled four, Hinton Rettiger came into the sheriff's office with a pad of writing paper under one arm and a stub of a pencil cocked behind his ear. Breathlessly, he surveyed the room. Whitelaw sat at his desk. The county prosecutor, Eugene Maher, stubbed out his cigar on the edge of White-law's spittoon. The two deputies, Drayton and Donimiller, were ranged on either side of the sheriff.

There was an air of expectation as the men stood in the presence of the lawman who had called them together.

Maher stood erect. "Welcome, Rettiger. Just in time for the biggest story of the year. Only because it's not an election year."

"And you're not running for anything," Rettiger said. To Whitelaw he said, "What's happening, Claude? I came as soon as I got your message."

"Macklowe's brother Reede has stirred up something with a couple of John Strickland's riders—a duel of some sort. I can't allow that to happen." He got to his feet and limped around the desk. He leaned back on the desk with his arms folded at his chest. "You haven't heard anything about it, Mr. Rettiger?"

"Not a damned word. Haven't spoken to either of the Macklowe boys since this morning after our game broke up. There were some bitter words exchanged at that time."

He looked at the lawyer. "What are you doing here, Gene?"

"Same as you, Claude called me. As an officer of the county court, I represent the people of Saint Mary and am charged with protecting their rights. We cannot allow thugs and shootists to disrupt the life of this community."

"Nice speech, Gene," Rettiger allowed, scratching on his pad with the pencil stub, transcribing the attorney's words. "You always did make good copy. Hope I'm still around when you make governor. Lord, imagine the speeches then—to fill entire issues of the *Mercury*!"

"Hinton, contain yourself," Maher said. "Claude needs us to keep our heads at a time like this. It's likely nothing at all will happen, but in the event of civic unrest we must be prepared to assist the law. Enough of your sarcasm. A small dose goes a long way, sir."

Eugene Maher was a relatively new resident of Absaroka County, having emigrated there from Albany, New York, less than a year earlier and having been appointed prosecutor by the territorial governor almost immediately upon his arrival—there being an acute shortage of lawyer stock in the vicinity.

He was a man of average height with a big barrel chest and a large head capped by neatly combed sandy hair. He dressed impeccably for all occasions, and this day he wore a gray wool suit and polished black half boots. Already, in his forties he displayed a comfortable paunch and a ruddy flush in his cheeks that evidenced more than a few ample meals that included the finest wines available in the territory. Here was a man with a big political future, as Rettiger was quick to point out.

Not that Claude Whitelaw gave a damn about politics— or the future, for that matter.

Whitelaw felt the pain in his legs as he stood before these men; they were not really his friends, but they believed, as he did, in law and order, and each was in a position to help him enforce the peace. Whitelaw experienced a wave of exhaustion that washed him from head to toe. He was getting too old for this sort of thing. Perhaps now was the time to turn the job over to a younger man, a man like Ben Macklowe, who had brains and guts and common sense.

But Ben Macklowe also had a brother named Reede, who was the cause of the immediate crisis.

"No law has yet been broken," Whitelaw said.

"But the intent has been announced by both parties," Maher said. "I'm surprised you haven't heard about the challenge that was thrown down, Hinton."

"I was printing the latest edition." He held up his ink-blackened hands. "I must say I am not surprised, after the acrimony at the card table, but we all left the hotel without any threat or challenge that I am aware of. As much as my profession causes me to pry and probe into others' lives, by nature I am a private man who likes nothing better than to mind my press and read my books."

Rettiger was, at least in his own mind, removed from, if not a bit above, the others in the sheriff's office. He looked down upon this mortal struggle from a rather lofty intellectual peak.

Educated—"ruined," he liked to say—at Oberlin College in Ohio, southwest of Cleveland, he kept a library of Latin and Greek classics in his bachelor quarters behind the newspaper office and printshop, and there he filled his active, incisive mind with the ancient writings that, he believed, were as alive as yesterday's three-column headlines.

Plato was his favorite, the philosopher who postulated a world of ideal forms corresponding to every object and idea on the quotidian plane of men. It thrilled and inspired Rettiger to contemplate these perfect forms or Platonistic ideals, especially in the realm of politics and government, where, he believed, the true nature, the best and the most venal sides of the human spirit, were made manifest.

Lofty, indeed. But here in Whitelaw's office the issues were much more mundane and immediate: there was going to be some shooting in Saint Mary, and the sheriff wanted to stop it.

"Well, you know this Reed Macklowe as well as anyone in town, which, admittedly, is not very well. But you have had drinks with him, played cards with him," the sheriff said to Rettiger. "Go talk to him. Tell him to stop this thing before it gets blown up out of proportion. And Mr. Maher, I want you to go to Strickland, talk to him, see that he reins in his boys. Nip this damned thing in the bud. And we don't have much time. Will you do this for me, gentlemen?" His brown hands clasped the edge of the desk and he pushed himself upright.

Rettiger said, "I'm no diplomat, Claude, but I'll do what I can.

"Mr. Strickland understands the law," Maher said. "He will see the necessity to prevent this ill-conceived 'show-down.'"

Both men left the office to conduct their peace missions. Whitelaw turned to his deputies.

"Donimiller, you'll be stationed here for the remainder of the afternoon and evening. I expect if there's anything I need you for, I'll get word to you. Drayton, you'll stay with me, go where I go, side me if it comes to any fighting."

Donimiller said, "Yes, sir." In his quiet and efficient way he was a very good lawman, a bit green yet, but willing to listen and learn.

Drayton stood a bit taller, threw his shoulders back. "Whatever you say, Sheriff." He was the more seasoned of the pair, a few years older, bolder, with a sense of humor and a sense of daring. The only drawback Whitelaw saw was that he was married and a father. Sometimes that sort of tie could hold a man back. He understood this and did not think it had affected Drayton's judgment yet. That would come—if it came—when Drayton was older, a bit more settled and mature and had seen more of the randomness of violence in the world.

For now, neither deputy had been jaded or worn down

by too many years wearing a badge or carrying a service revolver or tipping their hats to elderly ladies at community socials. That, too, would come, in time.

"Come on," Whitelaw said to the deputy, "we'll get some coffee." He put his gray hat on and hauled himself out the door.

JAIN SERVED THE TWO MEN A SIMPLE MEAL OF SCRAMBLED eggs and fried ham with fresh-baked bread, butter, and currant jam. Ben ate heartily, but Reede merely rearranged the contents of his plate.

"Got anything to drink?" he growled at Jain without looking up.

She went to the cupboard and pulled out an unopened bottle of whiskey. Jain looked at Ben, who shook his head in disgust. She placed three glasses on the table, filled them. Ben Macklowe took his drink, swallowed it, replaced the glass on the table. Jain sipped hers.

Reede ignored the drink in the glass and put the bottle to his lips.

Reede Macklowe was an angry man. He could not remember a time when he had not been angry: he masked it much of the time with liquor and bonhomie and moving from one place to another and never letting anyone, including his brother, come near him. Always he was riding away after inflicting damage upon himself or others.

It had happened last time in San Antonio several weeks ago. Before that it had been right here in Saint Mary, where he thought he would have the run of the town since his brother was a newly minted lawman. But there had been something different about Saint Mary: it was the girl, Dorothy Lewis, who had touched him, gotten under his skin. She had been the first in a long, long time to do that, and now she was gone. He had come back to see her, planning to take her away, but she was gone. She couldn't wait any longer for him—for anybody.

That made him the most angry, losing her, losing his

chance—as he saw it—at starting over, maybe making a life for himself this time. . . .

"I pray for you everyday," she had said to him as they lay in her narrow bed after making love.

"Don't waste your time," he said.

"You are a good man, Reede, but you don't want anybody to think that. You want everyone to be afraid of you."

"Who told you?"

"Nobody told me." She stroked his lean dark face. "I want to be with you, Reede. Please let me."

"Hell, I want you with me, too, girl. Only problem is, I don't know where I'm going. It's not so bad here—my brother's here and all. Nice little town, mountains, good people. Maybe we could just settle here."

Dorothy wiped her tears on the sheet. "Not here—they know me here. I want to go someplace and start fresh where they don't know I was—where they don't know what I was."

"Honey, you're a pretty little girl, that's all folks will know about you, and that's all they need to know."

He gathered her in his arms and she clung to him, her face against his hairy chest, breathing in the smell of trail and sweat and whiskey. He had been out looking for a ranching job. He had not found one yet.

"You know those McTiernans are a pretty high-handed outfit. The old man is obsessed with what he calls squatters on his half a million acres or whatever the hell he claims to own. The sons are no better—they jump when he barks. I don't know that I'd want to work there even if they offered me a job. Pay is lousy: twenty-two dollars a month, but you do get three squares, nice bed, good horses, Christmas Day off."

"Oh, Reede, you can find a job anywhere. Let's go away from here—far away. Start over just you and me."

"Honey, I want to have a stake before I light out. A man's got to have something he can call his own."

"You have me," she whispered, kissing his neck.

"Yeah, I do." Reede Macklowe pushed her back onto

the bed and rolled atop her small frame. He mounted her and savagely loved her.

Dorothy lay beneath him, dry-eyed, praying that she would conceive his baby, that her life would change—that he would take her away from this place forever. . . .

I killed her. I killed her, Reede thought as he pushed his meal away and brought Jain's bottle to his lips. Of all the things he had done in his life, this caused him the most regret. He would not show it to Ben or to anyone else—it was none of their goddamned business—but he would make them pay, by Lucifer—they would pay.

Jain cast a worried glance at Ben. He rose and went with her to the bedroom.

"What is wrong with him, Ben? He's acting very strange."

"That's just him. He's a brooding sort, just like our old man. I've got to be careful, though, that he doesn't get too much booze in him right now—might make him too wild to control."

"I'm worried, about you more than him," she said.

Macklowe kissed her high brown forehead. "I'll be all right."

Just then there came a knock at the front door. Macklowe went to answer it, passing Reede, who sat gloomily in his chair, unmoving, unseeing.

It was Hinton Rettiger. "Afternoon, Ben," he said, removing his battered brown hat. He stepped in. "Miss Dobbie," he acknowledged with a slight bow. He worried the hat brim with his blackened fingers.

"What do you want, Hinton?" Ben asked.

"Came here from the sheriff's office, Ben. Mr. Whitelaw asked me to talk to your brother. He doesn't want this shooting business to happen. You understand, Ben, you're a deputy sheriff. Saint Mary cannot tolerate it—bad for the town, bad for the county, bad for the territory. We're trying to make this a good place for families and ladies of quality to live." He gestured toward Jain, who stood near the stove listening to Rettiger, with one eye on Reed Macklowe.

The latter sat at the table as if he were a marble statue, his skin white, eyes glazed, not a twitch or any indication that he heard what was going on around him.

Ben Macklowe said to Rettiger, "You are right, of course. I'll persuade my brother to call it off."

"Maher went to talk to Strickland to put a muzzle on his boys," the newspaper editor said. "If he's smart, Strickland will send them out of town to sleep off their hangovers. Well, I'll report to Mr. Whitelaw that there will be peace in the streets."

"No such goddamned thing."

Macklowe and Rettiger turned to the source of the statement: Reede sat glaring at them with red eyes, his hands shaking, his jaw working to form words.

"I'm going to meet those two reptiles in fifteen minutes and they better be there or I'll find them."

"Don't be an ass, Reede," Macklowe said. "You heard what the man said: Whitelaw wants the whole thing called off, so we'll call it off. That's all there is to it."

Rettiger looked uncertainly from Reede back to Ben. "What should I tell the sheriff?"

"Reede and I will go to the office and talk it over with Whitelaw ourselves—right, Reede?" He stared at his brother, daring him to answer differently.

Reede turned his attention to Rettiger, ignoring Ben. "You tell the sheriff he better stay out of my way."

"You're talking crazy," Ben said.

Rettiger said, "I better report to Mr. Whitelaw. If Strickland keeps his dogs at bay, there won't be any trouble anyhow."

Reede Macklowe unleashed a loud, chilling laugh that was more of a howl, an expression of evil and violence. He threw his head back and showed his yellow teeth. "Ha! You don't know what the hell you're talking about," he taunted.

Jain came over to Ben, held his arm. She looked up into

his sad eyes; she had never hurt for him as much as she did right now as they watched his brother disintegrate before their eyes. She hoped he would somehow disable Reede and haul him off to the jail before he did any more damage to himself or others.

Rettiger stepped backward toward the door. He did not know that to say. He was frightened by Reede's bizarre behavior, afraid the madman would pull a gun right here and mow down the three of them who stood there like tin cans in a row awaiting a marksman to begin target practice.

Ben said, "You better get back to Whitelaw, Hinton."

"I'm on my way." Rettiger said. He put his hat on and bolted through the door.

Ben turned to Reede. "You are drunk and you are insane. You ought to go somewhere and sleep it off, son."

"Don't you call me son, you arrogant bastard," Reede snapped. "You're no better than me; we come from the same stock and we're going to the same grave. Just because you wear a badge now—"

"Shut your face," Ben said. "You don't know what the hell you're talking about. You come crawling back to Saint Mary and expect me to greet you with open arms? After what happened to that poor little whore? After all the trouble and grief you caused last time you were here. And now you want to play out some bullshit vendetta against a couple of ignorant cow riders and cause the entire town to pay attention. You make me sick."

He turned to Jain. "I apologize for my brother; you should not have to put up with this in your own home."

"I just don't want you or Reede to get hurt," she said. "He's drunk, Ben. He needs to sleep it off."

Reede slumped over the table, drunk, exhausted from spewing so much venom. Ben went to him, helped him to his feet, and the two staggered into the bedroom. Ben emerged a moment later.

"I put him down on your bed. You'll have to wash the sheets when he leaves."

She smiled and kissed her man. "I've got work to finish next door."

"I'll go speak to Claude, put an end to this thing. Would you mind if I came back for supper later tonight?"

"I will be very disappointed if you don't" she said.

CHAPTER 10

He heard the tolling of the hour as he approached the courthouse. He had not slept in a day and a half and it was wearing on him. For the first time in his life Macklowe felt old, and he wondered if Jain saw him that way. He was going to be a father, and he had not had time to experience the great joy that news ought to bring.

In his crossdraw rig, snug against his left rib cage, he carried a .44-caliber Colt's revolver with rubber grips. He wore a long canvas coat and pulled his black hat down tightly on his brow. He carried gloves in the pockets of his coat, but it was not yet cold enough to wear them; tonight it would be, though, when the sun was long gone and the wind curled around the mountain and washed through the streets. Winter was coming fast, and Macklowe did not look forward to it.

He strode purposefully up American Street in the long early-evening shadows.

It was only a few minutes' walk to the courthouse. He went inside and met Donimiller who was at the desk.

"Where's Sheriff Whitelaw?" he asked his fellow deputy.

"Out with Drayton. I'm stationed here for the night. Mr. Whitelaw expects trouble."

"There ought to be no trouble now. Has he spoken to Strickland?"

"He sent the lawyer, Maher, to talk to Strickland."

"Maher is a good talker, give him that much. He and Strickland will get along fine. I worry about those two hothead outriders, though."

Before the words were out of his mouth, Drayton burst into the sheriff's office. "Macklowe, where's your brother?"

Macklowe looked over Drayton's shoulder to see if Whitelaw was there. He was not. "Reede is sleeping it off at Jain Dobbie's house. Where is Mr. Whitelaw?"

"He's at the Stockmen's Club with Maher and Strickland. Trouble is, no one knows where Pearce and Brawley are."

"Jesus Christ!" Macklowe spat. He went to the rifle rack in a back room and took down a .44-caliber Evans New Model carbine, a repeater with a twenty-eight-shot magazine capacity, a sleek, unusual frame shape, and a twenty-two-inch barrel. This centerfire repeater used a special one-and-a-half-inch shell, and Macklowe put ten of these into the magazine and a handful into his coat pocket.

Out front he said to Donimiller. "Stay here like the sheriff told you. Drayton, you get back to the Stockmen's Club pronto, tell Mr. Whitelaw I'm going to bring Reede in for protective custody. Those two crazies might be out by Miss Dobbie's house. If I'm not back in twenty minutes, you get your butt over there. Understood?"

Drayton said, "Yes, sir," and very nearly saluted.

Macklowe pulled his coat open and stepped through the door. Now the wind was kicking up. It blew his coattails up as he walked around the corner, heading back toward Jain's place.

An ice-cold intimation of disaster gripped his gut. He stopped in his tracks and looked up. Across the street Pearce and Brawley were watching him. He took one step back toward the sidewalk.

Neither of the two cowboys wore a coat. They had enough alcohol in their veins to keep them plenty warm.

Brawley called out to Macklowe, "Where's your coward brother? We've been waiting for him. It's past four."

"He's not coming. He's sick in bed. You two ought to go sleep it off. Mr. Strickland doesn't want you out here anyway."

"What does Strickland have to do with anything?" Brawley growled.

"He pays your wages, man. He has some say in this. I suppose he even wants you to ride away from Saint Mary in one piece."

"You talk tough, like your bully brother," Brawley said. "I'm tired of listening."

"You're just plain tired," Ben Macklowe said. "I suggest you go see Mr. Strickland yourselves—hear it from him—then hit your bedrolls."

The two conferred in urgent whispers, confused and angry at Macklowe's words. Macklowe noted that each was armed with a pistol, and Pearce slung a Hood double-barrel shotgun under his arm.

Macklowe cautiously looked to his right, to see if Whitelaw or Drayton was within earshot. He saw no one. He took another careful step back until his heel touched the sidewalk. There was not obvious cover within ten yards in any direction. He was an unobstructed target. The rifle in his right hand felt suddenly heavy, and his palms were wet with perspiration.

Pearce and Brawley straightened and stood shoulder to shoulder.

"One Macklowe is as good as another!" Pearce called as he raised the Hood scattergun.

Brawley lifted his own pistol from its scabbard.

Macklowe stood stock still for a split second, then dived to his left, hitting the ground hard, as the shotgun exploded. Hot pellets bit into the street where he had stood, kicking up a dust storm as the shot echoed through the town square.

If there were any unsuspecting citizens about before the shooting, they immediately found shelter.

Brawley took three shots at Macklowe with his handgun, but he had terrible aim, and the slugs tore into the earth as Macklowe rolled first to his right, then left. His coat was laden with dust as he sprang to his feet and ran a half a block to seek cover around the corner of the building from where he had first walked.

Then, from the other end of the block he heard a familiar voice: "It's me you want, boys—and here I am!" It was Reede.

Macklowe could not see him from his present position. "Reede—what the hell are you doing?"

"Saving your life, brother!"

"You armed?"

"I have your old Spencer, and my own belt gun."

The Spencer was one of the most widely used models from the era of the Rebellion: Macklowe's was a .50-caliber seven-shot repeater with a twenty-two-inch barrel; it had been altered by Springfield Armory with a small swivel device forward of the trigger to allow for use as a single-shot. Macklowe had carried this one in Maximilian's army.

"Where's Jain?"

"She's safe."

Brawley and Pearce peppered both enemy positions with pistol fire. Macklowe ducked behind the corner of the building. Again he looked back toward the courthouse. No sign of Whitelaw or Drayton yet.

Ben Macklowe hefted his Evans and took aim at Pearce's shoulder. He squeezed off a shot, missed.

Pearce spun backward in panic and hit the boardwalk with a thud, drunk enough to feel no pain from his broken ribs, then jumped back, revolver in hand, and sent three quick shots at Macklowe.

Meanwhile, Brawley kept Reede pinned down where he was. Pearce stopped to reload and Macklowe tried again to wing him—he didn't want to kill the man. A .44 slug tore away a piece of Pearce's shirt, but the cowboy reloaded without pause.

Macklowe saw an opportunity. He leaped up and began to run in front of the building toward his brother's position.

Confused and distracted at first, Brawley held his fire.

Pearce yelled, "Blast him!"

Brawley had time for two quick shots that flew wide. Pearce by this time was loaded and joined in, creating a dangerous cross fire. Macklowe kept running: ten yards, seven, five . . . He dived beside his brother as bullets chewed into the sidewalk and the building. One ricocheted across Reede's face, deeply creasing his left cheekbone. Immediately it began to bleed.

Ben Macklowe righted himself. He saw Reede's injury and inspected it, pulled out a handkerchief, and held it to Reede's injured face.

"Look what you caused," Reede said.

"You're the one caused this whole damned mess," Ben hissed. "Hold still. You're stinking drunk. I thought you were sleeping it off."

"I wasn't really asleep. I heard you talking to Jain. She's a nice girl, Ben. Hope you can keep her."

"You know less about women than you do about cards," Ben said. "You're a goddamned ignorant, wrong-headed madman, and you're going to spend some time in jail when this is finished. Inciting a riot, assault, resisting a law officer."

"Now when the hell did I resist—"

"I told you to stay in bed and you disobeyed me."

"You are my little brother, for God's sake."

"Oh, I forgot to thank you for saving my life."

"You're welcome." Reede took the handkerchief and held it to his bloody cheek.

Macklowe peered around the building. Pearce and Brawley were just waiting for someone to show his face. They opened fire again. Thank God they were lousy shots.

"You know, we can just run back around this block and get to the courthouse in one piece. Then I'll lock you up and you'll be safe."

"Not on your damned life," Reede muttered. "These two clowns nearly assassinated you. They're going to pay for that."

"Look, it's all a misunderstanding, Reede. I'll hold up the white flag and we'll stop this thing. We'll even let them think they won."

Without responding, Reede eased himself onto his knees and lifted the Spencer to his shoulder. Pushing Ben out of the way, he lined the rifle and took two shots. With the second he hit Brawley and sent him spinning back.

Pearce ceased firing and looked after Brawley. His friend had taken a slug in his upper left chest. It had torn through muscle but not bone or artery. He was hurt pretty bad. His friend was shot, maybe dying. Pearce shocked sober, winced with pain from his own cracked ribs and almost started crying.

An eerie silence descended upon the scene as the wind stopped for a moment and dusk settled. Only a narrow gilded streak of sunlight limned the mountain to the northwest and the now cloudless sky hung like a pristine bowl over the town.

Ben Macklowe called out, "Your man needs help, Pearce. I'm coming in. Hold your fire." He stood.

Pearce panicked and emptied his revolver at the dark figure of the deputy sheriff. Macklowe hugged the wall to his right, prayed that Pearce's hand was shaking. It was.

"Don't be stupid, brother," Reede said.

"Shut up and stay put," Macklowe replied. "I'll disarm him and call you. When I do, you come help me lift the other one. He looks pretty bad from here."

Deliberately, Macklowe walked into the middle of the street, his Evans gripped loosely in his right hand, balanced perfectly parallel to the ground. At a second's warning it would be at waist level and firing—if Pearce got cute, which he did not think would happen.

For a moment he felt a chill up and down his backbone at the thought of Reede there behind him with a loaded repeating rifle aimed God only knew where—at his back? But the thought blew away as soon as it came. Not Reede. Not his only brother.

Several steps brought him even closer to Pearce, who

looked to be in shock: cradling his injured friend in his lap, tears in his eyes.

"Neddy, Neddy. . ." he moaned.

"Pearce," Ben said.

Pearce looked up, eyes glazed, like a coon shocked by lantern light. He said nothing.

"Let's help your friend to a doctor. He'll be all right, but he needs help."

"You killed Neddy."

"Nobody's killed nobody." Macklowe stepped up onto the sidewalk. "Let me have a look."

Across the street Reede hugged the wall of the building and watched Ben kneel to examine Brawley. Reede's head pounded and he felt dizzy. He'd been drunk for an entire day and for a moment didn't know where he was, but he snapped back to consciousness when he thought he heard something move close behind him.

He turned, saw a figure approaching him with a pistol raised. He shouted, lifted the Spencer and shot once, twice, at point-blank range without aiming, feeling the backfire of the powerful rifle.

The figure, a stout man wearing a gray hat, fell to the street.

Then Reede heard voices: Drayton appeared around the corner behind the downed man. "My God! He shot White-law!"

Reede looked up and saw John Strickland at Drayton's side. Both men looked at Reede, who turned and ran across the street where Ben was with Pearce and Brawley.

Ben had disarmed Pearce, and Pearce stood with Brawley in his arms.

"What happened?" Ben called.

He saw Reede stumbling toward him. Then over Reede's shoulder, he saw Strickland and Drayton. Those two raised their rifles and fired. Reede sprawled in the street, then scrambled to his feet again and made it to Ben's side as the two across the street opened fire again, this time sending out a heavy volley.

"Macklowe!" Strickland called out. "Your brother shot Sheriff Whitelaw! You better put him under arrest immediately." There was a brief silence. "Macklowe—you there?"

"I'm here, Strickland," he shouted. Then, to Reede: "What the hell does he mean, you shot Whitelaw?"

"I didn't know it was him—didn't know who it was. He came up behind me, I thought—"

"I ought to put a ball through your skull, you son of a bitch."

"It was an accident, Ben, I swear it."

"Like hell an accident."

"They're shooting at me." Reede ducked as a bullet spanged into a wall over his head. "Help me, Ben. I have to get away from here."

"Macklowe!" This time it was Drayton. "Surrender the prisoner!"

"You're not going anywhere except to jail, goddamn you." Macklowe raised his pistol, held it at his brother's head, and almost pulled the hammer back. But he stopped.

"Let's both of us make a run for it, Ben. After a while they'll stop chasing us. We'll be safe in Utah. I know a guy there."

"You probably know a guy in every state and territory both sides of the Rio Grande, brother. It's not my way anymore. I'm sick to death of running. I'm here to stay." He thought of Jain and the baby.

With that brief distraction his attention wavered. Reede saw it and raised the Spencer's butt and brought it down on Ben Macklowe's head. Macklowe slumped to the ground.

"We're coming in, Macklowe!" Drayton shouted.

CHAPTER 11

THE WOMAN LOOKED OUT THE WINDOW OF THE CABIN and saw the clear, moonless night sky. She breathed in the cold mountain country air, then closed the shutters and locked them.

She turned to the table where her husband, his second wife, and five small children sat with their hands folded in prayer.

"Sit down, woman," her husband said. "It is time to thank the Lord for His gifts."

She sat to his right—the other woman sat to his left—and bowed her head as he prayed.

Her name was Rebecca, and she had been married to this man, Joshua Young, for nearly ten years, and she had given him three children, a boy and two girls. This was the sum of her life and she was unhappy. She did not know what she wanted, but she wanted something different than what she had.

Joshua Young was the young prophet who had been proselytizing in Saint Mary; he bowed his prematurely bald head and intoned, "Father, we are most grateful for the food you have given us this day, for the family, for the Word that sustains us. Please bless this food that it may strengthen our bodies for our work in Your name. Please bless Your church on Earth, restored by Your grace, that we may be faithful and holy in service. We pray in the name of Your Son, Jesus Christ. Amen."

"Amen," chorused the wives and children.

Rebecca busied herself serving the children. Her counterpart, Joshua's other wife Sarah, served the man of the house small portions of the pork roast, yams, and string beans, and a chunk of freshly baked bread. He always ate sparingly.

Rebecca watched Sarah, who was several years older, wider in the behind, darker, and quieter—more accepting of her lot, more grateful to be a part of Joshua's life and mission—than was Rebecca.

Rebecca was prettier; she possessed a head of honey-blond hair, a pink complexion, a pair of violet eyes, and a figure that made men take a second look on those rare occasions when she went into town with her family. She spoke her mind more often than did Sarah, who had been married before to a much older man, an elder in the mission church in Montana. Sometimes Joshua told her to be silent, punished her with his silence, and did not sleep with her.

Sarah had borne two sons for Joshua Young, making him the very proud father of five.

As he picked at the food he glanced around the table at his children: a gaggle of towheaded creatures, little arms and legs, now filling their hungry bellies after a day of work and study. Even the youngest boy, age three, was responsible for helping Rebecca and Sarah keep the house clean, and he was learning his Bible history with the rest.

Spoons and forks scraped and there was no conversation. Not at Joshua Young's table. The whale-oil lantern in one corner of the room glowed brightly over the family and the rude sticks of furniture they possessed.

The children all slept in this outer room and the parents slept in the back room. Sometimes Joshua would take one of his wives to his bed and the other would sleep out front with the children. More often these days it was Sarah who shared his bed.

Rebecca held a strong but quiet resentment against this woman who had taken Joshua from her, or who had at least taken a piece of him. As infuriating as he could be, the young man of God was a solicitous husband and dutiful lover. At one time she had loved him—when she had married him at seventeen—but now she was not sure she did.

After the meal Rebecca helped Joshua dismantle the table while Sarah washed the dishes with the girls.

He spoke to her: "Rebecca, what is wrong, why are you so sullen tonight?"

"Nothing is wrong."

"It is sinful to lie, especially to your husband. Tell me what is the matter."

Rebecca pushed a stray lock of yellow hair from her eye. "I don't know what it is, but I am unhappy, Joshua. I feel as if I am not a good mother or a good wife. I feel that you are unhappy with me. I even think God is displeased with me—but I don't know why."

"You lack faith. You must pray. Come to me tonight. Sarah will sleep with the children. We will pray together to rid your soul of this demon."

"I don't think prayer is the answer, Joshua."

"Of course it is! I tell you it is, woman, and you must heed me."

Rebecca did not say anything more as she continued to help tidy the house and prepare the children for bed; Joshua read to the children from the Book of Mormon and prayed with them.

REEDE MACKLOWE REINED IN THE BIG BUCKSKIN AND DIS-mounted, leading the horse across an apron of shale at the base of the hill. He followed the sound of a trickle until he found a stream several yards away, a dark cold ribbon of water. The horse drank and Reede drank and washed his face.

He felt cold and dirty and tired and hungry—and thirsty. This was not how he had hoped to spend the night: on the run without food in his belly or a bottle of whiskey in his hand. He sat on the bank of the stream near a tall sweet-smelling pine. There were needles and cones strewn all around him and he very nearly lay down to sleep, but he knew he must keep moving. They would be coming after him.

After he had rendered Ben unconscious, Reede had taken his brother's rifle and ammunition and run to the livery, where he saddled the buckskin and fled.

He rode into the hills west of town, where the buckskin stepped strongly and confidently through the rough country, across coulees and through dense underbrush, around rocky outcroppings and dark juniper thickets. There was no moon this night, and Reede could barely see his own hand in front of his face. He had been moving continuously for four hours or more when he finally stopped to let the animal blow. There was a long trail ahead, and he must keep the horse as fresh as possible.

Goddamn Ben Macklowe, he thought. Why didn't he come with me? There's nothing for him in that two-bit town.

Reede just could not picture Brother Ben as a lawman. It did not suit. He remembered the kid with the quick fists and the flashing eyes, always ready for a fight, always dreaming of faraway wars and adventures.

As a boy Ben had read the novels of Sir Walter Scott and pretended to be the heroes the Englishman had written about. Ben had always had a vivid, active imagination.

Of course, it was tough, growing up with an invalid mother and drunken father. Ben had taken a lot of the responsibility for his mother upon himself—and he took a lot of the blame for his father's drunkenness, too.

Reede laughed aloud, picked up a pine cone, and tossed it into the stream. The horse snorted, breath steaming from his nostrils.

He had no canteen, a limited amount of ammunition, no coat or hat, a single blanket, two rifles slung onto the creaky saddle he had lifted from the livery. In other words, he had nothing and very little chance to survive.

Unless he could get hold of some necessaries. This was the rim of McTiernan country. But it would be foolish to go anywhere near the ranch house—word of Whitelaw's killing would have reached there by nightfall, surely. Strickland would see to that.

He would look for a line house. The McTiernan outfit would have a few in the foothills.

Reede took another drink at the stream, gave the buckskin a vigorous pat on his long neck, and mounted. He pulled the animal around to the northeast and followed the streambed for three or four miles, hoping not to leave too much sign that would be easy for a skilled tracker to follow. He fought to keep his eyes open and his mind off the screaming need for a drink.

"Well, old son, would you look at that," he whispered hoarsely, halting the horse.

Ahead in a small clearing on a green table of land was a small cabin. Too big for a line house, and there was light escaping from the shuttered window.

The events of the past day rushed in on Reede Macklowe. He relived the smoky card game, the hangover and the drinks he took trying to chase that away, the confrontation with the emaciated cowboys in the bar, his argument with Ben, the shooting . . . the shooting: he could not believe it had happened. He had killed a man, the sheriff of Absaroka County, Ben's boss.

How the hell was Ben? he wondered. He hoped he had not hurt the son of a bitch too badly. He had given him quite a rap on his thick skull. But Ben would come through it okay. Ben always did.

He kneed the buckskin into a walk and approached the house. He did not call out. Something told him to take special care this time: not that he felt immediately threatened, but his gut told him to be cautious. He smelled wood smoke, mingled with the odor of food—somebody had just eaten a meal. Reede shook his head to drive out thoughts of food. That would come later, if there was no trouble waiting for him inside the cabin.

Ten yards from the house Reede dismounted, took up the Evans repeater, walked deliberately to the door. He stopped, listened, heard a man's voice. He quieted his own breathing; he heard the man reading from what sounded like the Bible, the words coming slowly and distinctly.

This was not what he had expected: tenants—or maybe squatters—on McTiernan land.

He went to the door and pounded twice, stepped back with the rifle leveled. There was a brief commotion within. Then the door opened and a young man peered out.

"What do you want?" he asked.

"I need some food and shelter for the night," Reede said, "and something for my horse."

"We have little enough for my family of five children and two women. You're welcome to share with us what we have. There is no need for the weapon. Come in."

Reede was not surprised at the man's hospitality, though he had braced himself for hostility instead. Often on the trail he had been invited to share with others at campfires or line shacks, and on a few occasions he had himself provided water or a meal to a stranger. It was only good manners "on the border."

He stepped inside and saw the two women—one a pretty blonde, the other an older, rather homely gal—and five little ones huddled in a corner of the front room.

"Evening, ladies," Reede said, reaching to doff his hat, remembering then that he did not have one to doff. It made him feel naked, exposed.

"Sir, these are my wives, Rebecca and Sarah. I am Joshua Young, at your service—and in the service of the Lord."

"My name is Joe Smith," Reede said, thinking it best to give a false name.

"Any relation, perchance?" Joshua Young asked, his eyes alight with a strange intensity.

"I beg your pardon?"

"Any relation to the prophet and first president of the Latter-day Saints? I am a missionary elder of the church. Some people call us Mormons."

"Oh—" The two women—wives—now made sense.

These were Mormon folk with their strange ways and stranger beliefs. Well, they were welcoming enough, and the younger of the women was pretty enough. Damn! Reede said, "No, I don't believe so. My family hails from merry old England, not a churchgoing clan."

"Well, just an odd coincidence." Joshua Young turned to Rebecca. "Bring a chair for the gentleman, put it by the stove." He ordered one of the boys to see to the horse. "The rest of you children, go to bed, sleep the best you can. I am certain our guest will not disturb you as he takes a bite. Sir, sit down."

Reede Macklowe took the proffered seat near the stove, still clutching the repeating rifle. His eyes followed Young into the back room, separated from the front by a sheet that hung from a rod. The two women busied themselves reheating the leftovers, trying not to stare at the bloodsmeared wound on Reede's face.

He then ate a good hot meal, his first in many days, and drank a big mug of spring water. He wanted coffee but remembered hearing once that the Mormons do not believe in coffee or strong spirits. He could do with a drink, but tried to put that thought out of his head.

He burped and said to Young, who had taken a chair near him as he ate and was reading in the Scriptures, "might I borrow or purchase a coat, Mr. Young? I lost mine in a sinful game of poker in Saint Mary last night."

"Sinful, indeed," Young said. "I will give you what you need before we send you on your way, Mr. Smith. I would do the same for the least of my brethren."

"Obliged," Reede said.

CHAPTER 12

BEN MACKLOWE REGAINED CONSCIOUSNESS THAT NIGHT IN a narrow bed in Dr. Robert Justich's office just a block from the courthouse. Jain sat quietly beside the bed, her hands folded neatly in her lap. The first thing he said was, "What happened to Claude?"

"He's dead, Ben," she said.

"Dear God, I had hoped it was a dream. That bastard Reede killed him. Where is he?"

"He got away, stole a horse, headed out to the hills."

Ben eased himself up on one elbow, but the noisy throbbing within his head forced him to lie back and keep still; Jain replaced the cold cloth on his head and it soothed the pain momentarily.

"The doctor said you have a concussion, Ben. You must lay quietly."

His mind was anything but quiet.

He must find Reede and bring him back to Saint Mary to face justice. Memories of the day's happenings tumbled madly into his consciousness, but above all he heard the shots that had killed the sheriff, his friend, the man he had served with in the War Between the States.

"Where did they take Whitelaw? I want to see him."

"To Pride's Funeral Parlor. Why do you want to see him?" she asked.

"I want to examine the wounds. See from what range he was fired upon. One thing Claude always said, look at the

95

evidence, and if a body is all the evidence you've got, then take a damned close look at the body."

Jain Dobbie shivered. She had never experienced such sudden, brutal violence as she had today. That Reede Macklowe was capable of murder, she had no doubt, for she had seen the rage boiling within him and she had heard the stories from Ben of their youthful exploits. But to live it was different, and altogether frightening.

She gently pushed Macklowe's head back onto the pillow and lightly soothed him with her cool hands.

Jain herself had grown up in St. Louis, the daughter of a black mother and white father whom she did not know, had never seen, and supposed she never would—if he were still alive even. Her mother had died when she was nineteen, leaving her penniless and alone in the city and forcing her to support herself somehow. She had found employment as a domestic servant at the home of a wealthy merchant near the riverfront. She had worked there for two years before she saved enough money to travel west—as far west as she could. She came to Saint Mary, as good a place as any, by accident, set up her laundry after a time in Miss Julia's employ, and began to make a life for herself on her own in this new country, and though she had been lonely, she was independent—and she liked it that way.

So when Ben Macklowe came along, Jain Dobbie had been supporting herself for a few years and had learned to live without a man. She had known men before him; she was a beautiful woman with creamy skin, thick dark hair, and deep brown eyes. But the men of Saint Mary had misunderstood her, thinking that because she lived alone and had her own business, she was loose.

She needed love like any woman, but she had been waiting for the right man; and in Macklowe she thought she had found him—or that he had found her. He was quiet, strong, attentive, gentle but insistent in lovemaking. They could talk, they could laugh together.

As she sat beside his bed she thought back to the times they had spent together, the simple things they had done:

rides in the wooded hills, picnics, trout fishing in the cold mountain runoffs. Ben Macklowe had fought in two wars and was tired of conflict. He wanted a woman who demanded nothing but appreciated the fact that he treated her with warmth and dignity. In Jain Dobbie he had found such a woman. The more he gave to her, the less she asked from him.

Now, lying between Justich's starched white sheets with his head very nearly bashed in by his own brother, Ben Macklowe was as helpless as a puppy, and Jain was with him—where she wanted to be.

"Did Matt Drayton take care of those two banged-up cowboys?"

"He did. The doctor patched up the one and Mr. Strickland is putting them up at the Stockmen's Club. They're both probably fast asleep by now."

"They tangled with Reede, God help them. I wish I could have stopped it—the whole damned thing. I cannot believe Claude Whitelaw dead, is all. He was as much like a father to me as anybody ever was—more than my own old man ever was."

"Just be quiet, Ben. Don't talk. Don't think about anything. Drayton and Donimiller will take care of everything. They're good boys." She smiled at him. "Maybe I can move you into my bed and keep you there for a nice long time. I'd like that, Ben."

He scowled. "You'll have to tie me down, woman."

"You're not going anywhere tonight."

"I've got to find Reede."

"He won't get very far in a day or two. Besides, Strickland is going to talk to Mr. McTiernan about putting together a posse to go after him."

"Jesus!" Macklowe raised his hand to his throbbing head. "They can't do that. If they find him, they'll lynch him, simple as that. Even though he murdered a man, he deserves a fair trial."

"Please, Ben, stop worrying about it. Just get yourself better."

There was a shuffling at the door to the doctor's office, then a knock, and Gene Maher, the Absaroka County prosecuting attorney, came in, removing his hat with a distracted gentility he must have learned in the parlors of the homes of the finer families of Albany, New York. Maher sweated and his cheeks were even redder than usual, which was pretty red, and his unknotted tie spilled out of his rumpled coat. Lawyer Maher had been through a trying day.

"Mr. Macklowe, how are you?" He did not wait for an answer as he turned to Jain and acknowledged her presence. "Miss Dobbie."

"Maher, any word from the deputies about Reede?"

"They are staying close to home, and they ought to. Strickland is trying to organize some men to find your— that is, to apprehend the suspect. As the county's duly elected officer of the court I have issued a warrant for his arrest and deputized Strickland."

"Don't let a mob go after him," Macklowe said, each word an effort to form. "They'll not bring him back alive."

"Oh, I have advised Strickland to take every care not to harm him. He must be alive to stand trial."

"I'll bring him in," Macklowe said.

"You rest easy, friend. You're not going anywhere for a while." Maher took out a cigar and began chewing on it. "I have called an inquest for day after tomorrow. I hope you will be fit to testify."

"I'll be there."

Maher turned to go, then stopped and came back to Macklowe's bedside. "I have something that I was supposed to give to your brother, Ben. I never got the chance to do so. I shall entrust it to you, and you will see to it that Reede gets it when they bring him in?"

The attorney handed Macklowe a letter, than left.

Macklowe opened it. "It's the girl's letter—to Reede. Miss Julia didn't destroy it after all. She gave it to Maher." He looked at Jain.

She said, "I hope he gets a chance to read it."

Justich came back a little while later and examined Macklowe again, pronounced himself guardedly pleased, and allowed the head-injured deputy sheriff to go if he promised to get into bed and stay there, no arguments.

Macklowe swore on a Bible he would do just that, but he, Jain, and Justich all knew it was a lie.

REBECCA COULD NOT TAKE HER EYES OFF THE BLOODY furrow on the left cheek of the handsome rider who had polished off two heaping plates of food. Sarah watched her rival's every move and gesture and furtive glance with the intention of reporting to Joshua, their husband, the younger woman's untoward fascination with this uncouth stranger.

Rebecca did not know this. All she could see in the house was Reede Macklowe, known as Joe Smith, tall and trail-weary, a threatening presence yet somehow vulnerable, like a frightened fox fleeing the hounds.

Joshua Young busied himself with his reading and writing, on which he spent at least an hour each night: studying the Scriptures, recording his thoughts and the number of souls he had brought into the fold. His bishop expected a monthly report of his evangelical activities, and Joshua was nothing if not meticulous in his record keeping.

Joshua Young believed with all his heart and soul in the church and in his mission to be a fisher of men. He was serious, earnest, pious, and persistent. Just the sort of man the church required on this spiritual frontier.

Sometimes his devotion to church matters made him oblivious to the goings-on in his own home. This night, he was lost in spiritual considerations and forgot, for a brief time, that a stranger was present.

Reede, after he finished his meal, sat back in the straight wooden chair, his rifle leaning against a wall only an arm's length away. He could not take his eyes off Rebecca Young. The children were bunked down on the floor on the far side of the room, and the other woman, Sarah, attended to them before she disappeared into the back room where the young preacher was. Reede caught Rebecca's eye. Silently he signaled for her to come to him. She did.

"More water, ma'am, please," he said.

When she reached to take the glass from him, he touched her hand, held it for a second, and she let him. She gazed directly into his eyes and her soul touched his.

She was afraid, and she trembled as she returned his refilled glass to him. She wanted to say something but did not know the words. Her breath became shallow and difficult, her chest constricted painfully.

"Come here, girl," Reede whispered hoarsely, looking toward the back room to see if the other man or woman were watching. She stepped closer to him.

"You are real damned pretty," he said very softly. "I like you. Do you like me?"

Rebecca said nothing, couldn't move her lips.

"Just a little bit? I'm not a bad man. I'm running from the law, but it's not my fault." He did not know why he was confessing this to her, but it seemed natural. She took a half step closer and he smelled her earthy scent and wanted to take her. "I killed a man," he went on, "but it was an accident. Even my own brother doesn't believe me. I need someone to believe me."

Her heart pounded so loudly in her ears she was sure Joshua would hear it. She said, "I believe you." She put her small work-roughened hand on his cheek. "What do you want me to do?"

He said, "Just hush your mouth. When I signal to you, will you be ready to help me?"

"Yes," Rebecca said, her eyes aching from the brightness of the glow around this man whose name she did not even know: her savior.

CHAPTER 13

MACKLOWE SAT THE STRAWBERRY ROAN IN A DRY WASH with limestone walls. It was morning and the air was frigid. He stopped to light a smoke with a sulfurhead match from a secure steel canister. He leaned the heel of his left hand against the cantle, sat back, smoked and listened and looked around him. He had picked up Reede's sign outside of town, followed it for several miles already, and it was just past sunup. His head throbbed, and he still wore a white bandage around it, upon which he had fitted his low-crowned black hat.

The horse was from the sheriff's department remuda, and was a long-legged, white-stockinged gelding that had the chest for what promised to be a long ride ahead.

In a saddle scabbard he carried a new rifle, a Winchester Model 1876 in .45-75 caliber with a twenty-eight-inch octagon barrel. In his belt scabbard he carried a Colt's .45 Peacemaker and a hundred rounds of .45 cartridges in a leather pouch also attached to his belt. He hoped to God it would not come to shooting between Reede and himself.

In his coat pocket was the letter Maher had given him: the letter Dorothy Lewis had written his brother before she took her life. He had read it three times and it had sickened him to see the evidence of a wasted life and to know that Reede had been at least partly responsible for the despair that drove her to it.

In the dark hours before dawn he had gone to the funeral

101

parlor, awakened Pride, the dolorous mortician, and looked at Claude Whitelaw's body.

The sheriff lay there on a wooden platform a pale gray mass, his bent leg even more shriveled than it had been in life, his jowls sagging unnaturally, his eyes closed tightly, and the strong arms lifeless, upturned to show the hairless, fishbelly white undersides. The chest was sunken, the belly puffed, the testicles curled and shrunken, the knees knobby and scarred. This was the same Claude Whitelaw who had shown such unconcern for his own life so many times in war, who had brought back purpose to Macklowe's life and given him direction and stopped him from drifting, who had put aside the ten years of drinking and helling and urged Macklowe to do the same. The man who had, in more ways than one, saved his life.

Macklowe pulled the damp white sheet back and closely examined the gunshot wounds. There were two: one in the chest, below the right nipple and probably just an inch or two from the heart, a clean black hole; the second had hit square in the gut, a larger entry wound, perhaps because it had been at slightly closer range and taken more flesh with it, uglier than the first.

There was no doubt that both had been taken at point-blank range.

How the hell could Reede have been so stupid? Or so vicious? Macklowe still debated in his mind which it had been. Either one made Whitelaw dead.

He touched the corpse. It was more than just cold; it was stone cold, like the wall of a cave that had not been touched by sunlight in a thousand years. Whitelaw had been a man, and he was no more, only a lump of cold flesh that would soon crumble to dust and become a part of the earth once again.

He was too dry to shed a tear for his friend as he replaced the sheet and kissed the head through the cloth.

After visiting the funeral parlor, he had stopped by Jain's house for a change of clothes and received a reprimand from her, which he had to ignore. She was angry with him, as he knew she would be, but there was not a thing he could do about it.

Then he checked in at the sheriff's office, where both Drayton and Donimiller were keeping vigil. They were glad to see him up on his feet but expressed their doubt that he ought to be riding out so soon after the injury. He selected the rifle and revolver and signed a receipt for the strawberry roan and told them if they had not heard from him in three days to come looking.

It felt good to be out now, away from the town, even though as he rode it had been difficult to focus his sight clearly due to the head injury. As he sat on the roan and smoked, he felt more alert, awake, alive than he had all morning. He put the picture of Whitelaw's body out of his mind.

There was more than enough to concentrate on at present in tracking Reede.

Reede was a clever man, drunk or sober. But he had to be hurting—without proper clothing or supplies, food or water, other than what he could locate on the trail—and nothing to drink, unless somehow he had been able to obtain a bottle to take with him. And he had been without sleep for two nights running. He was like a wounded coyote, all the more stubborn and cunning and dangerous.

Macklowe did not look forward to finding him, but hoped he did before the posse that Strickland was putting together.

After he had left the sheriff's office and saddled the roan, Macklowe had made a final early-morning call in Saint Mary. He went to the Stockmen's Club and knocked on John Strickland's door.

The cattleman had tried to catch a few hours' sleep but apparently had not been successful. He was gaunt and unshaven and dressed in the same clothes he had worn the previous day. It seemed as if no one in Saint Mary was getting any sleep these days.

"What do you want?" he said to Macklowe.

"To talk."

"Seems we did that yesterday. Did neither of us any good then. Doubt it would now."

"Maybe not, but I want you to know I'm going out after my brother. I will find him and bring him in—alive. He will stand trial for what he did."

"Why don't I trust you, Macklowe? Is it because he is your flesh and blood? Or because I think even you can't bring the son of a bitch in without spilling his brains on a rock somewhere? Something about this whole thing smells rotten to me."

"What he did was wrong. I tried to stop him. He stopped me instead." Macklowe pointed to the bandage on his head.

"You're in no shape to be riding after anybody, and you know it. I will have half a dozen men on fresh mounts on his trail before noon. We'll get to him first, and if we can't bring him back alive, we'll bring him back in pieces."

"All I can do is ask you not to do this, Strickland. It's not because he's my brother, but because the law has to be observed. I want him to stand trial and to face the people of his town—not as a lynch mob, but as a jury. He will pay for what he has done."

"One way or the other he will end up dead," John Strickland said simply.

"One way is legal, one way is not."

"Same result." Strickland turned and went back into the room. "We both want the same thing, you and me. But I don't have any sentimental feelings about it. If you were in my position, you'd do the same thing."

"And if you were in mine, you would, too."

"Yes."

Macklowe dismounted and carefully extinguished the cigarette and buried the remnants of it in the earth, leaving no sign of his having passed this way. He remounted and rode on, skirting a long hill, careful not to show himself above the rim, as the sun rose higher in the sky, cutting into the cold the night had left behind.

* * *

REBECCA YOUNG PULLED THE BRIGHT BLUE COTTON SCARF
more tightly around her neck and adjusted her sore rump in
the saddle, a single-cinch California rig, also known as a
center-fire rig—which Rebecca did not know or care
about. All she knew was that after three hours in the saddle
she hurt like she had never hurt before in places she had
never hurt before.

But she did not issue a word or even a sound of com-
plaint or discomfort. She had made her decision and she
was willing to live with it. Yes, she was frightened, but she
also felt strangely liberated, more alive than she had ever
felt in Joshua Young's house or growing up in her parents'
house. It was new and wonderful and scary.

Last night she had gone to Reede Macklowe when he
summoned her, asked him what he wanted her to do for
him. She knew instinctively that it would require her to
violate her marriage vows, and she was prepared to do so.

He had taken her hand from his face and whispered to
her, "I will go outside and sit just below the kitchen window. When your husband and the others are all asleep,
come to the window, rap on it three times, then let me in
the front door. I cannot stay here the whole night, and I
need food and clothing, anything I can carry. I also need a
pack horse. How many horses does your husband keep?"

"Two," she said, "An old mare and a three-year-old."

"Good." He looked directly into her eyes. "You will
help me?"

"Yes," she said without hesitation.

Reede bid good night and thank you to Joshua Young,
who came from the other room to shake his hand and say,
"The Lord God will take you into His care if only you ask
Him, brother. You see how abundantly He has blessed me."

Sarah lurked suspiciously in the curtained doorway,
watching Reede and Rebecca, her lips a taunt line, her eyes
brimming with righteousness.

"Thank you, brother, and my thanks to your women for
sharing such a good supper with a stranger. I will sleep
outside. I don't want to trouble your fine family."

"No trouble at all. Do you have enough blankets? It is a cold night."

Rebecca handed Reede two extra blankets as Joshua Young smiled benignly at her, pleased and proud of his pretty and generous young wife.

Reede went out and soon the house was silent. Rebecca lay beside her husband and Sarah slept in the other room with the children. After a time Young turned and reached for Rebecca, who gently but definitely rebuffed his conjugal advances. He was perturbed, tried again—and again she put him off. In the deep darkness she heard his exasperated breathing as he turned it over in his mind; then he decided to make no more of it and, with a low grumble, turned his face away from her, to the wall. In several minutes she heard him snoring gently.

Joshua was a heavy sleeper, but she waited another half hour before she made the slightest move. Then she slipped out of bed and went to the window in the outer room and rapped it three times.

"What are you doing, girl?"

Rebecca Young jumped and almost cried out, but bit on her hand instead.

Sarah stood behind her, hands on her hips, a menacing scowl cut into her face. "Well—I asked you a question."

Rebecca, as she turned to face her adversary directly, reached behind and located a small iron skillet on the cold stove. She wrapped her fingers around it. She said nothing as Sarah took a step closer to her.

"Speak, girl. Don't think you are fooling me. I know what you are about. I saw you talking to that man. What did he say to you?" Another step closer.

The younger woman brought the skillet around and knocked Sarah over the head. Sarah slumped to the floor in a silent heap. Rebecca unlatched the front door and admitted Reede Macklowe into the house.

"Holy Christ, what's that?" he whispered urgently when he saw the woman's body on the floor.

"She tried to stop me."

"I hope you didn't kill her."

"I don't think I did," Rebecca rasped, praying that she had not. A new sense of defiance surged within her. "Let's do what we have to do."

As she rode the steel-dust gray three-year-old behind Reede Macklowe on the winding, tree- and rock-strewn trail in the cold dawn, she replayed the events of the early-morning hours over and over in memory. The gathering of supplies and clothing, stripping Joshua's gun rack of the two rifles, a box of ammunition from the bureau drawer, putting on two dresses and carrying the third, as well as her undergarments, in a battered valise. They had saddled the gray, packed the mare and tied her to Rebecca's horse, then set off without awakening Joshua or the children.

They had left Sarah lying on the floor unconscious.

Reede reined his buckskin around and waited for the girl and the pack animal to catch up. His senses were acutely alert to every sound and smell in this higher altitude; they had been climbing for two hours and it was not easy on the woman or the animals. Reede Macklowe felt fine, the best he had in weeks. He was on the move—going where he did not know, but moving, running. Today he was hunted: he could feel that, though he did not know who was following his trail. The town would send someone, perhaps one of the deputies and some handpicked riders. Whoever they were, he would outride and outwit them. That was the challenge, the thrill of it.

He regretted the killing of Sheriff Whitelaw. He had not meant to do it; it had been a reflex reaction during a firefight with the two mangy cowhands who had called him out. It had not been planned; it was not supposed to have happened. A man was dead, his brother and another man hurt, the town probably in an uproar about it.

But it was over and he must survive. He had a woman with him—also unplanned, unforeseen. Perhaps she would be useful; she had already saved his life. And she was the prettiest damn thing he had seen in a long time.

Rebecca caught up with him. A sheen of perspiration

lay upon her brow, trail dust smudged her face. She wore a floppy white hat she had stolen from Sarah, and it, too, was streaked with reddish dust from the hard morning ride.

"You holding up, girl?" Macklowe asked.

"Fine," she said, gulping for air, determined not to show the least weakness.

The two had not exchanged more than a score of words so far. It was more important to put the miles behind them. There would be ample time for talk when they stopped at midday for a meal and to water the horses.

"Come on then," he said, and urged his own horse into the climb. He looked back and smiled at her, his whiskers coming in dark and rough, his eyes burning with a peculiar intensity that sparked her very soul.

Rebecca Young shifted her bottom in the saddle, held the reins in both hands, kneed the gentle steel-dust again. The animal picked its way neatly among the rocks and fallen limbs that lay across the steep incline. The sun speared through elm and juniper and struck Rebecca's eyes as she climbed ever higher in the stranger's wake.

CHAPTER 14

PATRICK MCTIERNAN RECEIVED JOHN STRICKLAND IN THE study of the Big House on the MX spread. It was past nine o'clock in the morning, and Strickland had impatiently waited in the sitting room for over an hour, drinking coffee from a fine china cup and pacing before a man-high marble fireplace over which hung an oil portrait of the Old Man, Jack McTiernan, founder of the MX brand, in his prime.

The elder McTiernan son, David, was in Denver, Strickland had been told by the manservant who had ushered him into the sitting room. "Mr. Patrick will be at the Big House presently," the servant had said.

Well, here was Mr. Patrick, sitting behind the huge mahogany desk in the study, smoking his morning cigar, listening to Strickland's story. He was a tall, portly man, not accustomed to missing meals. His watery bluish eyes were set closely together beside a narrow nose in a broad face. His reddish hair was white at the temples, and his pinkish lips were thick and fluid.

He clenched the cigar in long yellow teeth. He said, "I thought this Macklowe fellow was a responsible deputy. Claude Whitelaw usually picks them good."

"He is, but the brother is a rotten one. A man cannot choose his brothers, Mr. McTiernan."

"Don't I know," Patrick McTiernan said, then burped.

As the younger son of Old Jack, this McTiernan had a reputation as a petty tyrant and skinflint. He kept the books

109

for the MX outfit, doled out the hands' paychecks, negotiated with buyers like Strickland, grudgingly paid the county taxes, and financed political campaigns for a chosen few in the territorial legislature.

The fortune Patrick hoarded had originally been accumulated by the Old Man himself, who had carved his empire out of these hills and valleys, fighting hostile Indians and equally hostile federal surveyors and bureaucrats. He had brought his first few hundred head of trail-tough cimarrones up from Mexico nearly a quarter century ago before the great drives. In the intervening years he had crossbred them with sturdier Texas beeves and imported a variety of shorthorns to gentle out the ever-expanding herd even more.

Jack McTiernan had worked his men nearly as hard as he worked himself, but not quite. Even in his forties he was known as the "Old Man," because of his autocratic ways and because of his steel-gray hair and lean, lined face. He left his wife and two sons in Santa Fe for several years until he had established his range and begun to build the first house, where he would raise the boys and keep his wife in style. She had hailed from Lexington, Kentucky, had been raised in quiet, scented gentility, and had been wooed by the slender, sinewy mountain-bred young man, who promised to make her the queen of a new empire.

That he had done, and for a few years Marjorie Cleveland McTiernan survived the harsh winters and dusty mosquito-hazy summers of the Big Horn country. She had died a decade ago, and the Old Man had remained housebound ever since, tenaciously keeping his clan close to him, having little to do with Saint Mary other than through hired emissaries, occasionally allowing one of his sons to travel to distant capitals, as David McTiernan was doing now, to conduct business that only a blooded McTiernan ought to conduct.

McTiernan's MX ranked among the great cattle kingdoms of the American West: at one time it had encompassed more than six thousand sections, or nearly four million acres of the finest grassland in the world, just on the upper northwestern lip of the Great Plains. All of it acquired and held together by the stubborn will and far-reaching genius of one remarkable man, Jackson James McTiernan, now in his eighth decade, a virtual recluse, a shadowy dictator—one of the most powerful men west of the Mississippi.

John Strickland took in the book-lined walls of the magnificent study of the Big House. As Patrick McTiernan puffed on his dreadfully malodorous cigar and droned on about how much money in "lost potential income" squatters cost his family, Strickland fixed on a trophy mounted on the north wall over a fireplace that was smaller but still as grandly constructed as the one in the sitting room.

It was a buffalo head—a white buffalo head—beneath which were crossed a broken lance and an old flintlock with a cherrywood stock and a barrel at least forty-six inches long. Strickland pondered the provenance of such a magnificent trophy and tried to imagine Old Jack McTiernan stopping a charging albino bull bison with the single-shot piece—or had he done it with the stone-pointed lance?

The more he learned about the elder McTiernan, the more interested he became. He pretended to pay attention to Mr. Patrick's ramblings.

"These parasites are very often criminals seeking to hide out from the law, and some of them even have the audacity to pass themselves off as 'homesteaders,' or to seek legitimate employment as ranch workers for the MX. Then there are the Mormons, a worse class, in my opinion, than the horse thieves and cattle rustlers; they seek to poison the minds of our people with their strange religion and anti-Christian practices. Multiple wives indeed! If my father were to encounter one of these adulterers, he would slay him where he stands, believe me, sir!"

"I appreciate all that, Mr. McTiernan, but I have a simpler and more straightforward task—to apprehend the killer of Sheriff Whitelaw. I have been deputized by the prosecuting attorney, Mr. Maher, and I came here to ask for MX men and permission to ride across your lands in pursuit of this murderer."

"Indeed. You shall have the fullest cooperation of the MX outfit, Strickland." McTiernan lifted a bell from the paper-cluttered desk and rang it twice. Within a few seconds the manservant appeared. "Fetch Red Colgan." The servant went out to accomplish Mr. Patrick's bidding. To Strickland, McTiernan said, "He is our foreman, a good man—if somewhat phlegmatic."

Strickland, who was not an educated man or a reader of books, was uncertain what the pompous Patrick McTiernan was trying to say. He endured several more minutes of excruciating monologue before the foreman arrived.

Red Colgan was a bantam with an oversized head that sprouted thick tufts of rusty hair, and his face was heavily spotted with orange freckles: over his forehead, across his nose, even onto his large ears. He stood erectly, his long arms hanging loosely at his side, his fingertips nearly reaching his knees. He wore an open-necked flannel workshirt, denim pants, mud-painted boots with small-rowled spurs. A greasy kerchief of an undeterminable color was knotted tightly around his neck. He held a battered brown felt hat in his right hand.

"Good morning, Colgan," Mr. Patrick said. "We have a visitor this morning: Mr. John Strickland. You may have met him before, he is a cattle buyer for an Omaha, Nebraska, firm. Mr. Strickland, this is Red Colgan, the MX crew foreman."

The two men shook hands. Strickland muttered a how-do-you-do; Colgan said nothing, but looked Strickland in the eye, unflinching.

Strickland then related to Colgan what the problem was and how he hoped the MX could help. Colgan nodded once during the recital, and when Strickland finished, he finally spoke in a reedy, high-pitched voice.

"I can give you four men and eight good horses, plus myself, and all the firepower you need, sir." He had the demeanor and inflection of a master sergeant reporting to his company commander.

Strickland liked what he heard. "When can you be ready to ride, Mr. Colgan?"

"In one hour, sir."

Strickland expected Patrick McTiernan to propose that the county reimburse the MX for expenses, but he said nothing of the sort. He mutely acknowledged Colgan's reply and gruffly put in, "Does that satisfy you, Mr. Deputy Strickland?"

"It does, Mr. McTiernan."

"Then you will excuse me, I hope. I have much business to attend to in my brother's absence. Please have some more coffee or something to eat while you await Mr. Colgan and his men. Avail yourself of the gentlemen's facility, if you wish. My father has seen that the house is equipped with all the most modern conveniences. He is a man who has always been ahead of his time. We have electric lighting bulbs and a telephone that only requires to be connected to the overland wire in Cheyenne. My wife purchased a pictograph machine in San Francisco recently for my daughters. It plays moving pictures. Quite amusing for the female mind." McTiernan rose ponderously. "Are you married, Mr. Strickland?"

"Widowed," Strickland answered.

"I am sorry to hear that. However, if you should be interested in remarrying, there are a number of eligible ladies in Absaroka County. You could do worse, much worse, Mr. Strickland. Good day to you, sir, and good hunting!"

When Mr. Patrick had been gone for nearly a half hour, the strange manservant came back into the study where Strickland had waited, sipping coffee. "Please come with me, sir. Mr. McTiernan should like a word with you."

"I thought we had said all we needed to say."

"Come, this way," the man insisted, showing Strickland into the hall and leading him up the wide staircase to the second level of the house.

It was not until they stopped before a tall white door that Strickland realized what the hell was going on. He had been summoned not by Mr. Patrick, but by the Old Man himself.

The manservant knocked three times, then pushed the door open and stepped silently inside. He stopped, beckoned Strickland to follow, then stepped aside. He announced the visitor: "Mr. Strickland, sir."

The visitor stepped forward into the murky room: there was no direct light from any source; the curtains were drawn, admitting only a faint glow of sunlight, and a shaded lamp burned in a far corner, several feet from the bed, which was a large island in the center of the room. On the bed, amid a rough sea of blankets, barely visible to Strickland as his eyes adjusted to the strange vision, lay a man, his upper body propped up on a whitecap of pillows.

The odor of camphor assailed Strickland, who choked back a cough. He was reluctant to step any closer to the bed, but the spectral figure raised an arm and with what seemed like an intensely concentrated expenditure of effort, beckoned with his hand for Strickland to come to him. This Strickland did, his chest constricting as his heart pounded violently.

"Did you wish to speak to me, sir?" he managed. He had never met the elder McTiernan before—and had never expected to.

Old Jack McTiernan moved his head. Cloudy wisps of hair barely covered the pink scalp that stretched tightly over his skull. His eyes shone with an inner light as they fixed upon the visitor. The raised hand, all bony fingers, remained suspended somehow in space.

Strickland shivered as the bedridden figure spoke.

"I killed the white buffalo with the spear, which broke as I drove it into his great heart. With that old musket I shot the man who wanted to take the trophy from me. I have killed men in my time, but God has forgiven me because I asked for His forgiveness." Each word received a breathless emphasis.

114

The speech took a tremendous amount of effort, and the Old Man's body seemed to shrink as he dropped his hand and lay in silence. Strickland looked around him. The servant was gone, the door closed. It was difficult to breathe, and Strickland felt a strange sort of panic—not that he was in danger, but that he was facing something he was not prepared to face: eternity.

The Old Man had read his mind. How? That, too, was scary. McTiernan, even in his weakened state, held certain powers, like an Indian shaman, and saw things from a different plane of existence. He had heard of such things but never seen the phenomenon firsthand. He stared at the shrunken image of a man in the bed.

"Your son is helping me pursue a murderer. We will capture the man and bring him in for trial."

"He will not come in alive," the Old Man breathed. "He will die. It is God's will."

"I do not intend to kill him—unless it is necessary."

"It is necessary that we die—all of us," McTiernan hissed.

"What do you want of me, sir?"

"Nothing. And everything. I want your youth, your life. Mine is ending and I do not want it to. I wish to defy God's will for me, and I will burn if I resist any longer. Do you know what it is like to be old, to be unable to walk or go out of a room like this?" The frail hand stirred at his side but did not rise. He could not move it again.

"Of course, you do not know these things. How could you? You know about business and 'justice' and young women. I used to live for such things. Now I live simply to breathe and to think, to communicate with God, and to watch my sons destroy everything I built. I wanted to tell you not to trust my son Patrick. He is an ass. The other boy is better but not strong enough. Strong father, weak sons. So it has always been through the ages. Would that I could reverse time and change—" He gasped for air. "So much that I would change!"

Strickland did not feel sorry for McTiernan; after all he

was a wealthy, successful man, feared and respected throughout the territory and beyond; but there was an aspect of tragedy in the Old Man's rantings. The founder of an empire had lived too long: long enough to see the administration of his vast holdings in the hands of men less competent than he.

Yet he had the spiritual yearnings of a monk. It was a paradox that Strickland was not prepared to understand.

McTiernan spoke again: "Who is this murderer?"

"He is the brother of a deputy sheriff named Ben Macklowe. Macklowe is a good man—the brother is rotten."

"Ah—so often that is the case."

"The brother shot Claude Whitelaw, the sheriff. I believe you knew Mr. Whitelaw, sir?"

"Yes, yes, a sturdy gentleman, a man of honor. He once turned down a bribe offered by my son Patrick. May God forgive my son and may He allow Claude Whitelaw the fruits of eternal joy in the realm of the spirit. I will join him soon."

He turned the glowing orbs—those eyes!—upon the visitor. He managed a ghostly smile, and Strickland saw the yellow teeth and dry gray lips.

"And yet I fear not. What have I to fear? Death? Ha! I have conquered death more than once." The frail figure moved almost imperceptibly and emitted a harsh rattle that Strickland interpreted as laughter. He had never heard the like before and hoped he never would again.

He gathered the nerve to ask the Old Man, "Why did you want to see me, Mr. McTiernan?"

Jack McTiernan gazed at Strickland without seeing him, then closed his eyes. His breathing became more labored, and it was apparent after a moment that he had fallen asleep.

Strickland went out of the room, closing the door behind him, grateful to breathe air free of camphor, age, and death.

CHAPTER 15

BEN MACKLOWE SAID TO JOSHUA YOUNG, "WHAT TIME did he and the girl leave here?"

"I don't know," the young preacher said. "In the middle of the night sometime. My wife tried to stop her."

He sat in the back room beside Sarah, rewrapping a wet cloth around her injured head. The children were huddled in the front room, aware that something was wrong, but not quite sure what.

It was noon, and Macklowe had followed Reede's sign to the Mormon's cabin, where he discovered Young and Sarah and heard their story of the stranger's visit and the disappearance of Rebecca.

Macklowe had fallen farther behind than he had hoped, but he was on the right track. He went outside to discover the missing horses and evidence of significant activity as Reede and the young woman saddled and packed the animals before they rode off due west into the mountains.

Ben stood upright and looked in that direction, following Reede in his mind. The man was insane to take the girl with him, that much was clear to Ben Macklowe. But that is how Reede always operated, beyond the boundaries of other folks' behavior. Ben seethed with anger, and his head ached as it never had before.

He returned to the house and thought it mildly comical, in Reede's destructive wake, that both he and Sarah Young had bandaged heads. She was not severely hurt because

117

Rebecca had not mustered too much force behind the blow with the skillet.

Macklowe spoke to the children, gently asking if any of them had heard the stranger leaving.

The eldest boy, the one who had attended to the buckskin, said, "That sure was a pretty horse the man was riding. Tall, like him. Sure was hungry, too."

From Joshua Young, Macklowe learned that Reede now was better armed, had a coat, plenty of food, a canteen, and cooking utensils. He was a more formidable quarry now—except that he also had the woman. . . . Ben could not puzzle that one out, hard as he might try. It was sheer stupidity on Reede's part. Nevertheless, this was how it was, and he would deal with it.

He thanked the Young family and went outside to his horse. The roan grazed outside the rude corral where Joshua Young had kept his animals. There were bits of grain strewn about, perhaps from yesterday's feeding of the mare and the three-year-old.

Just as Macklowe mounted, Young came outside. The sun stood near its zenith and beat down warmly upon the two men. But to the north gray clouds banked against the horizon. Young looked up at Macklowe.

"Bring my Rebecca back to me. God has already forgiven her, and I am trying to."

Macklowe reined the buckskin around and touched his hat. All this talk of God made him very uncomfortable. What was it with these people who lived in the mountains? Seemed they could talk of nothing else.

Their lives must be pretty damned bleak, he thought as he lightly touched the horse's flanks with his spurs. The buckskin surged powerfully through the underbrush as Macklowe handled him with confidence.

His entire body was sore now from the rugged morning ride. The stop at the Mormon cabin had been a respite, albeit a brief one, for man and buckskin. Now they must ride on to find the man. He turned back once when he had gone nearly a quarter of a mile through the scrub pine and saw Young and his remaining wife standing outside the cabin watching him.

As he climbed into the ever-thinner air of the mountain trail, Macklowe watched for signs of his brother and the girl, and easily followed in the wake of the three horses, one of which was laden with supplies, which was apparent in the heavier hoof impressions. One horse, probably the girl's, had a loose shoe on what looked like the front right foot. That would hinder their progress sooner or later, Macklowe guessed.

Of course, Reede would not check for a thing like that and take the time to repair it. He was in too damned much of a hurry—as always.

Since his mind drifted back toward the subject, Ben Macklowe wondered what God thought of his brother, whether Reede Macklowe was destined to be punished by an authority higher than the Absaroka County sheriff's department for his misdeeds on this earth; and Ben realized that there were probably many acts Reede had committed he was not even aware of. Hell, it was possible that Reede had killed several people along the way. Macklowe had no way of knowing—and Reede would be the last one to spill the facts unless he could gain some advantage from it. Macklowe smiled to himself, despite the gravity of the situation.

If there was a God, and Macklowe was not in any way convinced of it, then He must be having a great laugh over this one: the younger brother, who was no saint himself, riding after the "bad boy" elder brother, murderer and kidnapper, a thousand miles from where they had grown up.

Macklowe could not decide if he were riding to save Reede from Strickland's crew or Strickland's crew from Reede. The thin smile faded from his drawn face as the wind increased and blew leaves and brush across the trail. He bent lower in the saddle to concentrate on the sign.

For whatever the reason, he had better reach Reede and

the woman first—before the battle lines were drawn and retreat became impossible.

"IT'S GETTING COLDER," SHE SAID, UNABLE TO HOLD BACK her fear any longer.

Reede, five yards ahead on the tall buckskin, halted and waited for her to catch up. He rode around her and checked the pack horse. The supplies were secured properly and the animal was holding up. Better than he could say for the buckskin, which had begun to tire an hour ago. Reede had slowed the train, but had to keep moving. He was beginning to worry, figured this was as good a time as any for a short rest.

"We'll stop here," he said, looking around at the relatively flat table sheltered by fluttering aspens that caught the sunlight on their flat leaves and created a glittering shadows-and-light show—which neither Reede nor Rebecca could appreciate.

He smelled rain in the air and cursed silently. It was tough enough with the girl; a downpour would make it hell on earth.

She was conscious only of her own severe discomfort and fear. What had seemed like a romantic adventure the night before now was a very painful, very bad dream.

"Come on down, girl," Reede said, lifting his arms to help her from the saddle.

Rebecca had ridden like a man, no fancy sidesaddle for her, so she lifted her right leg over the horse's rump and fell into his arms, gasping at the exertion, her legs like battered sticks.

"There, you'll feel better after we have a bit to eat and something to drink. Wish your husband was a drinking man—not a drop of whiskey in the house," he groused.

"He doesn't believe in drinking spirits, says it is contrary to God's law. And the prophet Joseph Smith—the man with the same name as you—prohibited it among the saints. He spoke for God."

"Look, my name isn't Joe Smith, it's Reede Macklowe. I just made up a name so that your husband wouldn't be able to tell anyone I had stopped at your place."

Rebecca was puzzled. She had never known a man to use a false name. It smacked of dark intrigue—sin.

"Joshua would never hurt anyone who asked for his help. He is an honorable man."

Reede unpacked a kettle and skillet—the same one Rebecca had used to bang her rival wife over the head—and looked at her. "If you like him so much, why are you here with me?"

She followed him as he gathered dry sticks and brush for kindling. Overhead the sky grayed and the breeze became colder. She held her shawl securely around her shoulders. Rebecca said, "I thought you wanted me to come."

Reede said, "I like your looks, lady, but I'm not so sure you can keep up with me. I'm going places. They are not going to catch me and bring me back to that little hellhole of a jail and put me up for trial and hang me legal. It was a mistake is all, and nobody believes me—not even my brother. My law-abiding, law-enforcing brother! Now that's a joke. If they knew how many men he has stiffed and how many girls he has screwed—pardon my language, ma'am—and how many jails *he's* been in—well, they would not make him out such a big hero."

He hunkered to the ground and built a fire that soon crackled and burned smokelessly. He soon put two large dry logs onto the fire and sat back to watch them burn to coals. Rebecca meanwhile cut several strips of bacon and filled the kettle half-full of water from Reede's canteen.

"Is it going to rain?" she asked him.

"Looks like it."

The wind stung her face and caused the fire to whip wildly around the logs. Reede banked the little pit with rocks and dirt. He put the skillet and kettle in the fire between the large logs.

"What will we do if it rains?"

"I calculate we'll get wet," he said.

Rebecca Young was not used to such irony and such profanity. In her upbringing and her marriage, the language of the house had always been straightforward and godly. A surge of illicit excitement welled within her, blocking out the fear—for the moment.

She wiped the dust from her face with a handkerchief and sat next to him before the fire. "Aren't you afraid?" she asked.

"I have been in worse corners than this," he said. He got up and went to his horse. From the saddlebag he retrieved a handful of coffee beans, which he then dropped into the kettle that shortly began to boil and steam. "I suppose there are worse ways to drink coffee, but we are going to need something to keep us going at least until nightfall."

"I have never drunk coffee before," she said.

"I know, it's a sin. Well, young lady, you will have committed nearly every sin in the Big Book before midnight. I hope."

He looked at her and smiled his widest, winningest little boy's smile. In contrast to the gaunt features and the ragged bullet scar on his cheek, that smile worked wonders on women of all ages.

Rebecca's cheeks and forehead flushed a vivid pink. She was a damned good-looking woman. It was hard for Reede to conceive that she had borne three children, looking at that rounded figure, the narrow waist, long thin arms, and what he could only imagine were long, lithe legs.

"Now, don't you go getting shy on me, lady," Reede Macklowe said lightly.

"I have never been alone with a man other than my husband or my father," she said.

"That's going to change." He touched her chin, gently drew her face to his, and kissed her.

She kissed him back, passionately, fought his tongue with her own. She thought, I never . . . I never . . . then she let go of all thought and clung only to the feeling, the strong, strange sensation of kissing this man whom she did not even know.

Reede got to his knees, took her in his arms, then lifted her carefully and carried her to a spot close by that was sheltered by a tall limestone outcropping, where the earth was soft and smooth. He lifted her skirts and pulled down his own trousers, all the while his mouth molded to hers, and they coupled frantically as the horses snorted and stamped in the clearing. But they heard nothing except their own breathing, and they did not even feel the first giant raindrops that began to fall.

When they finished, Reede stood beside her and pulled up his trousers as she rearranged her clothing. He looked up and now saw the rain, heard the fire hiss as fat drops fell onto the red-hot coals.

"Let's eat, girl, and drink some coffee before it starts to pour down on us. Then we better get moving."

Rebecca followed him with her eyes as he walked back to the fire. She stood, straightened her skirts, and pushed the straw-colored hair away from her face. Her insides were churning with fear and pleasure. I never . . . she thought to herself with the faintest trace of a smile.

She put the shawl over her head and went to get something to eat and to be with him by the fire.

COLGAN SHOUTED TO STRICKLAND TO BE HEARD OVER THE hard-driving rain and wind: "They rode north from here!"

The manhunting party had stopped at the campsite where Reede and Rebecca had rested and eaten just a few hours earlier. Already the rocky ground was slick from the downpour that had continued unabated for at least two hours. And the heavy clouds darkened the sky much earlier than usual, making it that much more difficult to find the fugitives' sign.

"How far ahead are they?" Strickland asked Colgan.

"I'd say two hours, maybe more."

Red Colgan had served under Crook in the disastrous

Rosebud campaign several years ago. He had been a sergeant of scouts, commanding a squad of Indians who represented the Gray Fox's personal and particular style of warfare. It had proved effective in the southwest, but up north it had not worked so well. Crook took the Big Disgrace in stride, though he never forgave his commanders or the bureaucrats in Washington City for sabotaging his efforts to bring peace to the Montana country. In the years ahead he would once again campaign against his old foe the Chiricahua Apache in Arizona before he would be forced to retire from active service. And he was keenly aware that his defeat had paved the way for the Custer massacre and spelled an end to any hope of a moderate Indian policy in the region.

Strickland's party of six, including himself, had made rapid progress since they had left the MX after the noon hour and picked up Reede Macklowe's trail, thanks to Colgan's dead-sure tracker's instinct. Colgan rode point, with Strickland twenty to fifty yards behind, the rest of the men, all fully armed and supplied for a three-day hunt, strung out at Strickland's rear.

John Strickland was tired and felt sick from the cold and rain. The rain streamed in heavy rivulets from his hat brim and beat against his dark slicker and his horse's flanks. Through the mud his horse pulled him ahead, keeping pace with Colgan, who turned now and spurred his mount up the side of the mountain. The rain sheeted across the landscape and cut through right to the skin. Strickland kept his head down and held the reins loosely. He covered his rifle in the saddle scabbard with his slicker to try as best as possible to keep it dry. He wore two belt guns beneath the slicker as well. Each man in the party was similarly armed.

Try as he might, with the pressing matter of Reede Macklowe to concentrate on, he could not erase the image of Old Man McTiernan from his mind's eye. For some reason the frail figure in the bed—physically frail, that is, with a brain and a tongue as sharp as a razor—seemed to be right here with him, driving the hunting party ahead by the force of his personality, his steely will.

Strickland knew he was thinking crazy, that he should not be thinking at all but following Colgan and remaining alert to what lay ahead. He was convinced it would come to gunplay, that Reede Macklowe was not going to back down without a fight. Yet he was haunted by the unanswered question he had asked before leaving the Old Man. Why had McTiernan wanted to see him in the first place?

A chill ran through him, caused him to shiver, and his forehead broke out in beads of perspiration. He was coming down with a fever. Damn! He pushed himself erect, sat on the horse with determination not to give in until they had Reede Macklowe in sight. He would not fail.

Colgan, meanwhile, led the manhunt with a growing sense of excitement. He had picked up the murderer's trail above the MX boundary within a couple of hours of riding out from the ranch headquarters. His blood was pumping, his every sense attuned to the pursuit.

It brought back the nearly twenty years he had spent in the U.S. Army, from the latter days of the war, through service in Kansas, Colorado, and the Montana and Dakota territories, service as a horse handler and leader of scouts. He had seen his share of action on the so-called Indian-fighting frontier. But most of the time had passed with dull sameness in the gray barracks and on dusty parade grounds and in the stables of various posts to which he had been assigned.

He loved horses, treated them with respect, and he was considered the top handler at the MX, to whom the others looked for guidance. He was rougher on the men sometimes than he was on the animals. In that way he had earned their respect and ran a tight outfit, the best and the biggest in the territory.

Red Colgan sat his mount and peered anxiously through the pelting rain. He sighted a broken limb that might indicate Reede Macklowe's passage. He was curious to have discovered the tracks of three horses, one with a broken shoe that carried a light rider, the other heavily laden, undoubtedly a pack horse. Somewhere along the line the quarry had picked up a partner. His brother? Colgan did not think so: the second rider was much too light, like a woman or a child. Who could it be?

If he kept up this pace and forced his party to move ahead despite the downpour, he could catch up in a couple of hours, maybe less if Reede Macklowe slowed, if the horse with the broken shoe gave out.

Colgan kneed his mount gently and urged it forward.

CHAPTER 16

MACKLOWE DROVE THROUGH THE ICY RAIN, A BLACK specter, pushing his mount on as the trail became steeper and more treacherous. He cursed his brother and blessed his horse.

Wet to the bone, he rode against time into the increasing darkness. It was past sundown now, though the sun had not shown itself for several hours. The strawberry roan showed its blood, lifting the rider up the mountain, moving steadily without hesitation or fear, surefooted along the tortuous path.

Several minutes before, Macklowe thought he had heard a gunshot. It was difficult to be certain because there was the occasional rumble and crash of thunder in the valley, but this sound seemed so much closer and did not echo as violently as the thunder.

Suddenly the storm lessened, the rain became a black drizzle instead of a sheet. Macklowe sat the horse upright, creased his sodden hat. He felt better, felt a sense of hope that he had lost in the worst of the storm. Then he saw the little steel-dust gray's body in a ditch. He dismounted, went to inspect the dead animal. There was the front right hoof, cracked, shoeless.

Reede had killed the animal, probably taken the girl onto the buckskin with him, and God help the pack animal.

Macklowe felt close, very close. In fact, his scalp began to prickle as he sensed another human presence ahead on

127

the trail. He remounted, sore and tired and thirsty. He rode another half mile before he saw them, Reede walking beside the buckskin, the pack horse tied to saddle horn, the woman sitting the saddle but bent over in exhaustion.

The rain ceased as Macklowe came up within ten yards of the fugitives.

Without warning, Reede wheeled around, the Evans repeater in his hand, cartridge chambered, ready to blast his pursuer. Macklowe lightly pulled in the reins, gentled the roan to a halt.

"Ben, goddamn you, what are you doing out here?"

"Came to save your life, brother," Ben Macklowe said.

"You better worry about your own."

"Who is he?" Rebecca asked.

"My little brother," Reede said.

"You must be Mrs. Young." Macklowe moved out of the saddle, hit the muddy ground with both feet, not for a second taking his eyes off Reede. "Your husband wants you to come home, ma'am."

"She's not going anywhere, Ben."

"You have nothing to say about it. Look at her. She's soaked, tired, probably got the grippe. Give me the weapon and the other guns, Reede. We'll find someplace to make camp, build a fire if we can. Then we'll go back down in the morning."

"You alone?"

"Yes, but John Strickland has some men—I don't know how many—riding with him. Don't know how close they are, but I'd wager they're right on your trail—and mine."

"Should have killed him when I had a chance," Reede muttered.

"No more killing, brother. I am going to take you back to Saint Mary to a nice warm jail cell, where you will await the circuit judge and trial. That is the only thing left to do."

"And let them hang me like a common criminal?"

"You are by no means common, Reede. You are a Macklowe like me. Remember what Mama always said about the Macklowe clan? We are more trouble than we are worth, but we are worth more than trouble."

"Clever woman," Reede said to Rebecca, helping her off the buckskin but maintaining his grip on the rifle.

"Maybe we better go back with him," she said, trying not to burst into tears, grateful that the rain and the terrible climb were ended. She had made up her mind hours ago: she was going back to Joshua, no matter what sort of terrible punishment he meted out. She just wanted to go home. It seemed very far away from this place.

Reede stood back and again lifted the rifle barrel, aiming it directly at his brother's gut.

"We are not going back," he said.

Ben Macklowe stood next to the roan with his hands at his side, trying to decide if he should reach for his own rifle or revolver and challenge Reede's stupidity and stubbornness. There was not much time. He did not know how close Strickland might be and with how many men he was riding. And he did not want to take a chance, especially with the woman here. She was a complication, and Reede was well aware of the advantage of having her with him.

"Reede, there is nothing for her out here. Let's take her back to her husband before she gets hurt."

"Nobody's going to get hurt." Reede looked at the woman, then at his brother. He relaxed his grip on the Evans and eased the barrel down. "I don't bear you any ill will," he said to Ben. "As long as you keep the badge in your pocket we can talk like human beings."

"It does not work that way. I am sworn to uphold the law. Claude was a friend of mine. I would expect him to do the same if I was the one lying on a slab with two bullets in me."

Rebecca flinched; she looked at Reede Macklowe differently than she had before. This strange nightmare was becoming real to her at last. He did not return her gaze but held his brother's eye with his own in a dark challenge.

From behind Ben came the sound of approaching horses. Ben did not turn around. He knew who they were.

Reede went white, lifted his rifle once again. Rebecca froze in abject fear where she stood.

"Move," Macklowe said evenly.

Reede did not need to be told twice. He put the woman in the saddle and hauled himself up in front of her, wheeled the tired buckskin, and pushed it over an upgrade into the thick stand of timber that shadowed the edge of a narrow canyon.

Macklowe watched them go, then unbooted his rifle and turned to face the riders.

He saw Red Colgan first, leading the party. He had met Colgan once or twice in town, did not have a very good sense of the man except that by reputation he was quiet and contained and competent.

By now the drizzle had stopped and the air was gray and heavy and cold. That was bad because it would be easier to shoot—and shoot accurately—now that the rain was gone. Macklowe pulled out the box of ready-made cigarettes, put one in his mouth, and lit it. Damn, it tasted good and the smoke went right to his brain and cleared it of the terrible thoughts that Reede's stupid actions had put there: thoughts of massacre and mayhem.

He cradled the rifle in his left arm, gently pushed the roan out of the way. The horse sought a comfortable place to stand, long black tail switching. A good-looking horse, Macklowe thought. Hope it does not get hurt today.

So he stood alone, water dripping from his slicker, legs set apart, smoking the cigarette.

Colgan saw him, stopped, waited for Strickland and the others to catch up. When Strickland came up, he pointed up the slope to Macklowe. Strickland raised his hand. Macklowe raised his in reply. Strickland spoke to Colgan, then urged his mount forward. Colgan and the other riders stayed. Macklowe could see Colgan speaking to his men, gesturing calmly, making sure everyone knew his place if it came to fighting.

John Strickland was as wet as Macklowe. His face was drawn, his eyes sunken beneath the dark brow. This was the man who had slapped Macklowe, who had shared drinks with him, who now wanted the same thing Macklowe wanted: to bring Reede back to Saint Mary. But Strickland was a latecomer to the Reede Macklowe game. Ben had been playing it all his life. He was tired of it, but he was not going to turn his chips over to a stranger.

"Where is he?" Strickland asked.

"He is close by. I told him to make himself scarce for the moment. I told him I am going to take him back."

"That is why I have come. I am deputized by Maher."

"Of course, Maher would not trust me to do it."

"It is not a matter of trust, Macklowe. It is a matter of bringing the killer back, nothing else. Maher must have figured I could gather the men to do the job."

"He has a woman with him."

"That is a piece of bad news."

"I feel the same way. She is tired and scared, wants to go home."

"So do I, Macklowe. This is not my line of work."

"Why don't you and your men ride ahead. I will follow with Reede and the girl. We will get him to Saint Mary in one piece and make sure the girl gets home."

"I don't feature him riding behind me. He's well armed, I assume."

"I will take his guns. When we get to town, we can sit down and talk about what happened."

"We will settle this here and now." Strickland watched Macklowe toss the burning butt end of the cigarette into the mud. "I do not want to be hard about this, but I will be if I have to."

Macklowe looked up at the cattle buyer, who sat a tall sorrel mare with a white star on her face. Strickland was trying to do the right thing, but he was not Reede Macklowe's brother. That was what it boiled down to. As much as Ben respected Strickland's position, he could not see his own blood in someone else's custody.

"I will give you his arms and mine," Macklowe said. "Between here and Saint Mary we will ride with you. Once we get to town, I will take back my guns and his, and I will arrest him and lock him up."

Strickland considered this offer. He had come to view Ben Macklowe much differently over the past twenty-four hours, since their first decidedly unpleasant meeting at the Grand Central. Macklowe would be a good man to ride the river with, perhaps to partner in a cattle operation here in the Big Horn country. Strickland regretted losing his temper over some heated words at a card game, and he was impressed that Macklowe could put it behind him, stand here now and talk like a civilized man. Still . . . he saw the determination in Macklowe's flinty eyes.

"I will compromise. We take your brother's weapons, but not yours. You and I ride out front, let Colgan and his men guard Reede. The girl will be safe; we will get her home, no problem."

Ben's horse whickered and Ben looked over his left shoulder. He caught a glimpse of color, of movement, then he heard the explosion of the Evans repeating rifle. As he turned to Strickland he saw the man pull upright in the saddle, clutch his chest, then fall.

Below, Colgan circled his hand over his head and called to his men to charge up the slope.

In a nightmare moment of dread and anger, Macklowe looked at Strickland, who lay twisted in the mud. The hand at his chest was scarlet with blood, and blood bubbled from his gaping mouth. His eyes were open, staring at Macklowe, but there was no life in them.

"Ben, get your ass over here!" Reede shouted.

But Macklowe hesitated. Reede had killed again and was more desperate than ever now. Reede was on the wrong side of the law and would never be right again. Ben did not want to run anymore, wanted to stay clean and fulfill his sworn duty as an officer of the law. Then he thought of Rebecca Young. Someone had to look after her. He made his decision.

He turned just as Colgan's party opened fire upon him. He ran to the timberline, clutching his rifle, and dived behind the trees. There Reede awaited him, a smile of triumph on his scarred face.

"You stupid goddamned son of a bitch!" Ben spat.

"Watch your language, there is a lady present," Reede said.

A volley of fire ripped into their position. Ben Macklowe peered out and watched Colgan and four riders dismount and take cover behind rocks and trees about twenty yards down the slope.

Rebecca's dress was torn, stained with grass and mud. Her face was a mask of terror. She was slumped against a tree, a helpless rag doll. She looked at neither man as they ducked to avoid the withering fire that kept coming from the MX men. A stray bullet could easily hit her.

Macklowe crabbed over to her, forced her to lie flat against the wet, hard earth. She whimpered but did not resist. Then Macklowe went back to Reede's side.

"Give yourself up," he said, putting his hand on his brother's arm.

"You are in this with me now," Reede said with a crooked smile.

"No, I'm not," Macklowe said.

"Then what are you doing here?"

"I want you to give it up. I will be sure you get to Saint Mary alive. The killing must stop, Reede."

Colgan's crew fired only sporadically now, since there was no response from Reede Macklowe. They were wondering what the hell was going on.

Then Colgan called out, "Throw your guns down and come out! We will cease fire for one minute. After that—if you don't surrender—we're coming in."

"For God's sake, Reede," Macklowe pleaded.

"No damned way. Let them come."

"What about her?" Ben pointed at the girl, who still lay facedown, sobbing.

"She'll be all right."

"You can't be sure of that. If you make her keep this up, she will either die or run away. It's no good."

For a few seconds Reede said nothing. He pondered his brother's words. Then, without a word, he stood, lifted the repeating rifle, and began firing at Colgan's position. The assault took the MX party by surprise and there were shouts and return fire.

Reede Macklowe took a slug in his gut and spun back. As he fell another bullet creased his arm. He landed nearly on top of Ben, who pushed him over, inspected his wounds.

Macklowe shouted, "Cease fire, Colgan! He's hit bad. We're coming down."

Rebecca Young, scratched and muddy, her dirty face streaked with tears, scrambled to Reede's side. "Oh God!" she screamed. She pushed herself to her feet and ran out of the trees and down the slope toward Colgan, leaving Ben and Reede alone.

Reede's face was white, drained of blood. He moved his lips but no words came out.

"Rest easy, boy, we will get you to Dr. Justich. He fixed me up after you knocked me over the head."

A smile played upon Reede Macklowe's bloody lips. "I gave you—a—good one," he whispered with difficulty.

"Why are you such a hard case, boy?" Ben said. He took Reede's head in his hands.

"Made—that way—oh Jesus!" His face contorted in pain and his body spasmed. Blood flowed from the wound in the abdomen, drenching his shirt and trousers.

Macklowe knew there was no hope, but Reede could linger for another few hours. He had seen such wounds in the war and watched men die in agony, heard their screams, remembered them in his dreams.

He said, "I could kill you myself for all the trouble you have caused. Claude Whitelaw was a good friend, saved my life, Reede."

"Accident," the wounded man gasped.

"I believe you. But Strickland was no accident. You shot him down in cold blood."

Reede tilted his head, gazed steadily with effort at his brother. "Yes—I did—had to."

"None of this had to happen, boy. None of it."

Macklowe felt the tears burning in his own eyes. Reede's head was heavy, and Macklowe's arms and back ached from the effort of holding him. That summed up Reede: he caused pain to others, wherever he went, whatever he did.

"Macklowe! What is happening up there?" It was Colgan, getting restless.

"Come on up, Colgan. We are finished here." He looked down at his dying brother.

"Ben—" Reede rasped. "Finish it—please—finish it."

"I can't—" The tears blurred his vision.

"For me—one last thing—please—Ben."

Macklowe unholstered his revolver. He looked up and saw Colgan hovering there, rifle leveled at Reede. "Stand back, Colgan."

The MX foreman understood what was happening and did as Ben requested.

Ben Macklowe cocked his revolver. It weighed a ton, and he held it to Reede's head. His hand shook. Reede looked directly into his eyes, took a ragged breath, and smiled oddly. The blood foamed pinkly in his mouth.

"Good-bye—brother—"

"Good-bye, Reede," Macklowe said, then squeezed the trigger.

Absaroka County, Wyoming Territory . 1882.

Eugene Maher presided at the triple inquest into the deaths of Claude Whitelaw, John Strickland, and Reede Macklowe. It was found that Reede Macklowe had murdered the first two gentlemen, and that Reede Macklowe had taken his own life after being wounded by Red Colgan in a gun battle on the mountain.

Hinton Rettiger said to Ben, "Your family makes very good copy."

Ben Macklowe said, "Leave me alone, Hinton. Write what you want to write about Reede and the others. Reede was dead wrong; he crossed the line and couldn't come back to the other side. But just leave me alone."

"You going to stay on as deputy sheriff?"

"If the new sheriff wants me, I'll stay."

"Some folks say you ought to be the new sheriff."

"Some folks think I ought to be strung up in the square."

"You are being harsh on yourself, Ben."

"Am I?" He looked around the courtroom, saw Jain waiting for him near the door. "All I wanted when I came to Saint Mary was to find some quiet, a job I could do that would let me sleep at night. Claude Whitelaw made it possible for me to start fresh. Reede came damn close to taking it all away again. If I had stopped him, done something—I don't know what—"

136

"He was bent on self-destruction," the *Mercury* editor said. "No one could have stopped him."

"But I am his brother."

It was a cold November day and the bright sun slanted into the room through the tall dusty windows, throwing off motes of light and casting long shadows. Maher had finished his work and stood, puffed up like a governor, behind the bench talking to several of the town leaders. He looked a sure bet for some political gain from this.

Macklowe went to Jain. She took his arm, conscious of the stares and whispers of the ladies who awaited their men. She stared back, causing them to avert their eyes.

"Are you ready to go home?" she asked him.

"Yes," he said. "Home."

ABOUT THE AUTHOR

GREG TOBIN grew up in Independence, Missouri, attended Grinnell College, and graduated from Yale University. He is the author of STEELMAN'S WAY, JERICHO, and KID STARK, published by Ballantine. He lives with his wife and his two sons in New Jersey.